The Princelings and the Pirates

Book 2 of *The Princelings of the East* series

Jemima Pett

The Princelings and the Pirates
Book 2 in the Princelings of the East series

Cover by Danielle English http://kanizo.co.uk
Chapter illustrations by the author

Other books in the series:

The Princelings of the East
The Princelings and the Lost City
The Traveler in Black and White
The Talent Seekers
Bravo Victor

Blurb Edition 1.1

Princelings Publications
© 2012, 2015 J M Pett

This book is dedicated to
Diane and Mike, Clare, Dawn, Kate, Tonia, and all those
who gave me inspiration,
and not forgetting Jean and Geoff of Castle Fortune.

Contents

Cast of Characters

Fred and George: The Princelings of the East, staying at Castle Buckmore and working on their Philosophy and Engineering interests

Victor: barkeeper of the Inn of the Seventh Happiness, studying to improve his job prospects

Prince Lupin of Castle Buckmore: a prince with a problem

Baden: Lupin's steward

Vladimir: Fred and George's uncle, and steward of Castle Marsh

Lord Smallweed: second in line at Castle Vexstein, and practising his influence

Bailey: a journeyman at Buckmore, responsible and knowledgeable but not yet fully qualified. Acts as messenger quite often.

Harry Senior: the sommelier (wine expert) at Buckmore

Young Harry: a young person learning the trades of Buckmore, often sent on errands. Harry Senior's son.

Princess Kira: second daughter of King Helier of Dimerie, and a spunky young lady, not afraid of hard work. Not afraid of much at all, in fact.

Princess Nerys: first daughter of King Helier of Dimerie. Kind and helpful, and ready to do her duty.

Miles and **Morris**: Nerys & Kira's older brothers, Princes of Dimerie.

Frankie: a pirate on the Golden Guinea, likely to tell people what to do

Captain Starling: Captain of the Golden Guinea. Given to wearing a large hat

Pippin: a small pirate with a handkerchief on his head for stylistic reasons. Helmsman of the Golden Guinea.

Captain 'Feathers' McGraw, aka King Ludo of Marsh aka the Pirate King. Says it all, really. Oh, his ship is the Meerschweinchen or the Mare Swine. Wonder why he got a ship with a German name. Maybe it's Dutch?

Rum: red-headed pirate on the Mare Swine with a black eye patch. Quite helpful really.

Arthur: princeling of Humber with big ideas about himself

Theo: princeling of Wold with a rather clearer view of his status in life

FGP: secretary and general factotum to Uncle Vlad

Sundance: a person of mystery, generally thought to be in the Secret Service

King Lynn, Prince Hunston and Monty: King, Crown Prince and Steward of Castle Wash respectively

Robert: a major in the Western Marches army, in charge of the 25th Rifle Company, among others. Brother of Baden.

Haggis, Neeps, Baker and Chad: half the soldiers of the 25th Rifle Company

Prologue

In which we meet Princess Kira and she meets disaster with equanimity

"There's a noise of oars or something, I tell you!" Princess Kira turned away from the window where she'd been peering out into the mist. "I'm sure something's going on out there."

"But nobody's sounded an alarm, Kira. You've just got the jitters because it looks spooky out tonight."

Kira crossed the room and jumped into bed next to her sister, Princess Nerys.

"Oh, maybe," she said, shrugging her shoulders and looking at the window again. "You can't see a thing out there though. It would be a great night for them to attack."

"And just who is 'them'?" asked Nerys in a scolding tone. "You know Miles and Morris said there were no such things as pirates and the people on the shore were just being hysterical."

"Well, I don't know, but what they were saying about the wine being stolen and the vineyards being overrun sounded pretty much like raiders from the sea to me, and if that's not pirates, what are they?"

Nerys said nothing. Her sister had a good point there. Things had been bad for the past few weeks and her father, King Helier, her brothers and all the courtiers had been deep in discussions from which, on the whole, the two eldest princesses had been excluded. They'd been frustrated at not knowing the details. Usually their brothers kept them informed so they'd be well-trained when they eventually had castles to run themselves. For their husbands, of course.

Kira got out of bed again and returned to the window. Before she could get there it broke into hundreds of pieces and a leg appeared through it, followed by a body. More legs and bodies followed. The room seemed filled with large, smelly strangers with long smelly hair. Some of them had swords.

Nerys screamed and ran for the door. Kira didn't scream but ran for the door, which was not much use as a pirate beat her to it, although she saw Nerys slip through it and yelled "Run, Nerry" as hard as she could. She slipped under the arms that were trying to catch her and tried to get to the fireplace. Someone else blocked her path; hands were grabbing at her, some touching her, some just missing. It felt horrible. If only she could reach the fireplace! There was a secret exit there. Or behind the tapestry! No, there were two pirates in front of that. The room seemed full of them. She turned once more, trying to evade their greasy hands that marked her dress as she slipped from their grasp. She ran straight into a large blanket someone put over her head and then her arms were bound to her sides. She carried on kicking as many shins as she could, gaining some satisfaction from the grunts and 'oofs' emanating from whomever she connected with.

"OK, Missy," said an authoritative voice. "Ye can just stop all that now. We've got ye fair and square and we be takin' ye away. Hostage, see?"

She stood still, and drew herself up straight as a princess should, preparing to meet her fate with honour, whatever it was.

"Ye goin' to be sensible, now? Good. We heard ye was the sensible one."

The blanket was removed from her face so she could see her assailants. She thought about saying something like "Wait till my father finds out" but decided it would sound silly, so she just stared at the guy who seemed to be in charge and waited calmly, although she felt anything but.

"I am a Princess of the blood and demand to be treated honourably," she tried, and was glad to hear her voice sounding strong and serene.

"Yeah, honourably is fine by us. We'll be takin' ye hostage now, aboard our ship. It won't be too comfortable for a bit, but then you'll be well cared for when you get to where we're going. If ye behave, that is. Will ye behave?"

Kira nodded. She could hear nothing from the rest of the castle suggesting an alarm had been raised, or if it had, that anyone was coming to her rescue. She decided she'd better go with the flow and hope castle politics would come to her rescue. Or a knight in shining armour, she thought, with a slight smile which she stifled immediately. She shouldn't let anyone read her thoughts, and it wouldn't do to start thinking the ridiculous. "Focus," she thought to herself.

And like the true Princess she was, she allowed herself to be manhandled through the window, down over the rocks and into the boat below which transferred her to the waiting ship.

And set sail into the mist under a pirate flag.

Chapter 1: A Case of Wine

In which we discover more about Castle Buckmore and Prince Lupin has more than one problem

The wind blew over the meadows and through the trees, rustling the leaves turning red gold and brown as autumn spread through the land. The high hills beyond Castle Buckmore already showed a dusting of snow on their highest and most shaded slopes. Small machines whirred at intervals around the castle, each with three vanes catching the breeze, and they pivoted to show exactly which way the wind was blowing, recording their motion on a drum and pencil arrangement concealed in a box at the base.

Fred withdrew his gaze from the window, and returned, still deep in thought, to make some marks on a large sheet of paper covering half the floor. He sat back and admired his work, giving a small sigh of contentment. He wrinkled his nose as he became aware of a smell of slightly singed hair, and looked up to see his twin brother George watching him.

"How are you getting on?" George asked.

"OK," said Fred and he looked at George more closely. Despite the various bald spots on his back and sides and the marks where his hair had been singed over the summer months (and as recently as last week), he could not discern any new signs of explosions or accidents that might have befallen his brother down in his laboratory. In fact, Fred concluded, George was bursting with excitement and could indeed explode into the air if he did not let his news out very soon. "What about you?" he said nonchalantly.

"I've done it!" George exclaimed, and did indeed give a little hop and skip round the room as he came over to his brother.

"Well done you!" Fred said, patting him on the shoulder, "When can we tell everyone?"

"Oh, not yet!" said George, "I only mean that I've managed to get a controllable current – it lit up the light bulb, nothing exploded, and I even tried again with a switch in the circuit, and I could switch it on and off! It is quite stable!" And he hopped and skipped round the room again.

Fred smiled, and wondered if he dared say what had sprung into his head. He decided he could.

"I thought you were using strawberries, not currants."

George stopped and looked at him frowning. "Of course I'm using strawberries. I mean currents as in stream... Oh!" and he giggled as he realised what Fred was up to and they both dissolved into laughter.

"Aren't you a bit early though?" Fred said.

"Oh there's loads yet to be done, finding tolerances, making it a suitable size, designing appropriate vessels, working out how long the strawberry juice will last, that sort of thing," George replied. "It'll probably take a whole year at least."

"Well, you haven't got much more than a year, you know."

"I know," said George, calming down and looking worried again, "I'd better get back to work again."

"Oh, no!" said Fred firmly. "No, you are taking the rest of today off, if not the rest of the week, and we are going to celebrate and have a few days' holiday. It'll clear your brain for the next step."

The brothers were referring to the task George had revealed to Fred in the early summer, after they had successfully stopped the Energy Drain and laid the plans for the export of Vex ale in a few years time in return for the import of Wozna Cola. They had left their patrimonial home Castle Marsh, and come to stay at Castle Buckmore at the invitation of Prince Lupin and Lady Nimrod. Their hosts furnished them with a small apartment with an excellent view, so that Fred could continue Philosophising, and a spacious laboratory in the depths of the castle where George could carry on his Engineering. In the course of their adventure George had discovered that strawberry juice could be used to make a great deal of useable energy, and although he had worried whether he was free to make use of this knowledge, he had been assured that he was indeed the one who would reveal this secret to the world. There was even a date specified: January 2011. So here, in the autumn of 2009, George had made a breakthrough on his path to fulfilling his destiny.

"Oh, I suppose I can afford to take one day off," said George, going over to the window and looking out. "Perhaps we could have a look at the results of the wind mapping experiment."

"I'd love to," said Fred, "but I really think you should have a real day off, not just substitute one project for another. I'll get the recordings in at the end of the week and set them out, then we can look at them together when you have your next break."

George nodded. He would have enjoyed a walk to

get the recordings in, but more data would be very valuable, and he didn't really want to work on it now, his head was really too full of his strawberry juice breakthrough. His stomach rumbled and he wondered when he had last eaten, probably breakfast, he thought.

There was a knock on the door and a brown haired person with intelligent dark beady eyes stuck his head round the door.

"Baden!" said Fred welcomingly. "Come right in, you don't need to knock!"

Baden came in. He was Steward of Buckmore, a sort of general assistant as well as friend to Prince Lupin whom they had met on the earlier adventure. They had discovered he was a princeling from the House of Powell but had, like so many princelings do, given up his claim and was now effectively part of the House of Buckmore.

"I thought you'd like to know that Prince Lupin expressed interest in your well-being and asked if you would be attending dinner tonight?"

"Does that mean we've missed too many dinners?" asked Fred, rather astutely.

Baden chuckled. "Yes, but also Lupes has some news which he wants to tell us," he said. "You don't have to attend dinners, you know that, but apart from the fact he likes your company and likes hearing about your experiments, I think it helps you to fit in here with the rest of the household."

Fred and George exchanged glances. "Sorry, Baden," said George, "Yes, we will come to more dinners. I do enjoy them, except when I've got something on my mind."

Baden smiled again. "You are a mysterious pair, you know. Quite the guys of intrigue. Dinner is in about half an hour, in case you've lost track of time. What *is* that?" and he looked openly at Fred's paper at which he had been taking surreptitious glances the whole time they'd been speaking.

Fred laughed, "It's a combination wind and weather and topographical map." He said. "There's lots still to do to it. I keep finding interesting patterns in it. One of them put me in mind of a labyrinth the other day and I went off and looked up mazes and labyrinths in Buckmore's excellent library and forgot what I was supposed to be doing entirely."

"Have we got a library?" Baden asked, astonished. "Well, I suppose the old king or his father before him must have made one. I expect you're the only one who's ever been in there."

"Oh, I have too," said George. "And I saw Prince Lupin in there once, in the Heraldry section."

"Ah!" said Baden, with a twinkle in his eye as if he was sitting on a secret.

"And I saw him in the tax and finance section," added Fred, at which Baden frowned.

Just then a bell chimed three times. "Early warning for dinner," said Baden. "New idea of Lady Nimrod's. Are you ready and shall we go down straight away?"

They decided a quick wash and brush up would not detain Baden, so they did and then went down and up stairs and round corners, and then down and up more stairs to get to the Prince's dining room.

* * *

They were halfway through a very satisfying meal, discussing general events around the Castle and gossip from the travellers that had passed through when Prince Lupin, sitting at the head of the table with Lady Nimrod on his right, suddenly stopped in mid-sentence and looked at his wine, holding the glass up to the light.

"What is this?" he asked. "I've been trying to work it out all evening and I kept thinking my palate had quite lost me. Pass the bottle down, Baden."

As Baden did so, Fred, handing it on saw it had a label saying "Cavée", quite different from the usual "Chateau Dimerie" they drank on these occasions.

Lupin looked at it and called for the sommelier. The guests murmured among themselves while Lupin toyed with the rest of the food on his plate, obviously impatient for the castle's wine expert to give an explanation. With hardly any delay a wizened elderly person slid into the room and bowed deeply to Prince Lupin and his guests.

"Well, Harry," said Lupin, "What is this Cavée stuff and what's happened to the Dimerie?"

"My deepest apologies, my lord," said Harry, the sommelier, in a subservient tone. "At the last delivery we had a note from Dimerie apologising for the absence of any white wine due to a failure of the crop and a problem in the store which had reduced their stocks completely. They promised to send some from the second store at Fortune, but none has arrived. I sent the best of the other to you hoping it would satisfy."

"What's been going on there?" Lupin asked. "Have we checked?"

"I have heard nothing of any problems with the grape harvest," added Lady Nimrod.

"We sent a messenger, well actually my journeyman, young Harry, to see what was going on and to check any other whites that might be available, even if of inferior quality. I'm afraid he hasn't returned." Harry senior looked worried.

"How long ago did you send him?"

"Three weeks ago. And when he wasn't back in two weeks we sent a messenger, who should have returned at the very latest by this morning. So we sent young Bailey down to the Inn of the Seventh Happiness, giving him strict instructions to go no further but to check for any gossip there. He should be back by tomorrow lunchtime as we said he should stay overnight to get the best chance of news."

Lupin nodded. Harry senior had acted appropriately. He looked around the table. "What do you think?" and he looked first at Baden.

Baden thought for a moment. "It's strange," he said. "There were no reports of anything amiss earlier in the year, no problem of drought, or disease. I'm sure we would have heard something earlier, before stocks ran out. Besides, Dimerie would surely have warned us so we could spin out the best wine for special occasions, if there was any hint of a shortage to come."

There was general agreement on this, and as Lupin looked around the table, no-one had any further ideas to add. One or two made appreciative comments about the substitute wine, which made Harry look a little relieved that at least his judgement had not gone awry.

Fred and George kept quiet during this interlude, as neither had sufficient experience to tell the difference between the wines. George felt he rather preferred this new one, which the pair of them had occasionally had with one of their meals at the nice outdoor restaurant in the plaza near the castle entrance. But both were puzzled. Buckmore had such excellent communications, which included a very intriguing vacuum post that George hadn't yet had a chance to examine, as well as the exchange of messengers and general gossip, that this lack of information was very unusual indeed.

After Harry had left them, Lupin signalled for the sweet course to come and while they waited for it to arrive, he toyed with his wine glass, frowning and occasionally making a 'Harrumph' noise under his breath. They ate the sweet, an extremely nice summer pudding with blackcurrant garnish, in virtual silence, as Lupin's mood continued to dampen spirits. At last the meal was cleared away, a glass of mead was served all round, and Lupin looked up at them all.

"You may have gathered," he said, "that I brought you all here this evening for a particular reason."

Knowing looks were exchanged between a number of the household, and the others just continued to look at Lupin politely, or interestedly, or both.

"The argument has been pressed upon me," he continued, "and I have finally yielded, to the suggestion I should take a bride."

There was general murmuring, a few cries of "congratulations" and a lot more knowing looks exchanged. Fred and George wondered why this was an issue, as in their experience, it was only the king that actually had to get married, to ensure the line of succession.

"So," continued Lupin when the hubbub had died down a bit, "Baden has been looking for suitable candidates for me, and discussing them with Nimrod and myself, and over the next couple of months there will be a series of young ladies coming to visit me, and the castle, to see who □" he tailed off, almost embarrassed.

"... will be the lucky lady," completed Lady Nimrod for him. Lupin nodded, glumly.

Baden cleared his throat, his eyes twinkling with amusement. "H-hm, who will be the first to visit?" he enquired.

"Princess Ruby of Vexstein," Lupin replied morosely, clearly his mood getting worse the more he thought of it.

"... and when?" asked one of the other senior members of the household whom Fred and George had not yet met on a social basis.

"The day after tomorrow," Lupin sighed, his misery complete.

"Cheer up, Lupin," said an elderly person Fred had always liked, who reminded him of his own Uncle Vlad. "You have to pay some of the penalties for getting away with your charade for so long you know!"

Fred didn't quite know what to make of that, but it made everyone laugh, and Prince Lupin did actually manage a wry smile, and the conversation broke out again, with those on George's right talking about the eligible princesses that might visit the castle, and those on Fred's left, including Baden, returning to the issue of Dimerie's wine.

The party rose from the table and Fred and George followed Baden and his companions out on to the moonlit quadrangle where the night air was starting to carry a hint of frost in it.

"What do you think of this wine business?" Baden asked them.

"I don't know enough about wine or how it grows to say," said Fred, and George nodded in support.

"Well, I think there's something funny going on." Baden looked at them. "And I think you two need to go and take a look. I would come with you, but I'm not sure Lupin won't need my support for the next few days, with Ruby-booby coming."

"Ruby-booby?" asked Fred, wide-eyed, and he and George dissolved into giggles again.

"She's not the brightest girl in the world, but she's very sweet," explained Baden. "She's the most acceptable option presented by Vexstein, and of course we must honour Vexstein by considering her."

"Why does Lupin have to marry?" asked George.

Baden looked from one to the other, then somewhere into the distance. "I'll tell you later," he said, turning back to them. "Meanwhile, will you go and look at what's happening at Chateau Dimerie? I'll find someone who knows their way about to come with you. You are still very much of Castle Marsh, you two."

"You mean we haven't caught up with the ways of the world yet," said Fred.

"Yeah, just a little naïve. Although Young Harry is anything but, and something seems to have happened to him. So naivety might not be a bad thing in this investigation. You come to these things with an open mind – partly your training and partly lack of outside influences. Anyway, Lupin trusts you."

"What do you want us to do at Chateau Dimerie?" asked George. "I'd like to have just a little bit of a plan for this you know."

"I don't quite know," Baden responded. "Let's talk with Lupin in the morning, then go when we've heard from Bailey - actually he's a nice lad, you could go with him, unless Lupes thinks he can cope without me. I'd like to come. Dimerie's a great place and I'd be worried if they've got problems they feel they have to hide from us."

And with that, they went off to bed, Fred to dream of the wind blowing labyrinthine patterns through vine leaves, Baden to dream of the sea breaking around the rocks on which a castle stood, and George to dream of equations and strawberry juice.

Chapter 2: Fortune Favours the Brave

In which Fred and George take the Fortune-Dimerie Line

The carriage rolled to a stop in the market square at Seventh Happiness under a deep blue sky laced with twinkling lights strung across the canyon in which the settlement had grown up. Fred and George stretched and got out. Baden threw down his crossword puzzle in disgust and Bailey stayed sound asleep in the other corner, having had altogether too much travelling for one messenger in the last 36 hours.

He had arrived back at Buckmore just after noon, having ridden fast since early light. It was as well he had hurried as it enabled a brief planning meeting with Lupin, decisions to be taken, and the four of them to be bundled into the coach with a sketchy plan and some extra provisions.

Bailey had found little to report.

"I found no trace of Young Harry," he had explained, "although Victor, Argon's son, Argon that runs the Inn, he suggested Harry had gone down the Dimerie line just before they got strange reports of disappearances filtering through from Humber-Wash way."

Everyone had agreed that Victor (who had played a major role in solving the energy drain problem) probably had a better handle on the news than Bailey could have found out from him, and would be a useful addition to their mission. The general plan was to stay one night at the inn, then go down the Fortune-Dimerie line.

The Inn of the Seventh Happiness heaved with laughter, jollity and people generally enjoying themselves. Baden squeezed through the throng at the bar, trying to catch the barman's attention, while Fred and George found a table in the corner. They also found Victor, bustling about in his normal hyperactive way. They put in an order for two rooms, one at least, 2 Vexes, a Strawberry Juice and a Celery Spritzer (George confessed he didn't want anything to do with strawberry juice for a while) and a Melange du Jour for four, plus to let Baden know he needn't order at the bar. Victor bustled off and in a trice he arrived back with the drinks, and followed by both Baden and Bailey.

"That was good," said Baden approvingly, "Your health!"

They raised their glasses, completed the toast and sipped the drinks appreciatively.

Bailey spotted someone he wanted to talk to: "Comes from Humber," he said over his shoulder as he took his drink and walked off, leaving the Princelings together.

It wasn't long before the crowd began to disperse. A few took the night bus down the Corey-Vexstein line and some went on the sleeper to Powell, that was drawn by two very slow-looking animals rather than the smart horses Prince Lupin had for his coaches.

"I wouldn't like to go home that way," remarked Baden. "Slow and boring."

"But ok if you're asleep, perhaps?" asked George.

"Who is going to sleep with all that rattling around?" responded Baden.

"Maybe that's why they drink so much Vex before they go," laughed Fred.

Victor came over to them and cleared away the meal he had brought over earlier.

"I have two rooms. Not good ones, sorry. Same one as before," he said, looking at Fred and George, "And one joining Prince Lupin's usual room. It's in use, sorry."

"What would you have done if he had come here himself?" asked Baden.

"Erm, lady would have been given other quarters. Someone else move☐"

"Ooh, a *lady*," they chorused, emphasising the 'lady'. It seemed only Lady Nimrod was a well known lady traveller.

"Who is it? Not Princess Ruby?" asked Baden.

It seemed not, which didn't surprise Baden as she would hardly need to stay at the Inn with Vexstein only two hours away. Whoever it was though, Victor wasn't telling.

Fred and George said they were happy to take the cubbyhole, both thinking maybe they'd get a full night's sleep in each other's company this time, so Baden and Bailey went up to the small servants' room adjacent to the guest suite.

"What do you think we should do?" said Fred as he and George laid down for sleep. Having sat in the coach all day neither felt particularly sleepy even though it was getting late.

"I think one pair, including Baden, should go as

official visitors from Buckmore, concerned at the lack of news from Dimerie and also looking for their journeyman, and the other should go as normal travellers. The big question is, can we go together this time or do we have to split up again?" he said referring to their previous adventure.

"We are of one mind on this," replied Fred. "I really missed you last time and I wouldn't choose to split up. But do we know enough about how the world works outside Castle Marsh to cope with danger we don't know about?"

"We always lived on our wits there," said George. "Baden thought our naivety could be an asset. If we are two innocent tourists it will be all the easier to act as innocent tourists!"

They debated the point forward and back for a while, and whilst there were good reasons to split up, in their hearts they knew they just wanted to stay together on this trip.

"You know what we haven't done?" said Fred suddenly.

"Um," thought George, "er... invite Victor along?"

"Right," Fred said. "We thought it would be good."

"Invite me along where?" said a voice which was followed by a head poking up from a hole in the corner.

"How long have you been there?" asked Fred in exasperation.

"Not been there at all. Came along tunnel. Heard 'invite Victor along'. Asked question." Victor said.

The brothers grinned at each other in the dim light of the glow they had yet to put out.

"It looked busy tonight, Victor," said George, "but do you think you could come on a journey with us?"

"Oh yes," said Victor, "but must be back in three weeks. Course starts again then. Gandy's day off today. No help for dad."

"We need to set off in the morning. We don't know how long we're going to be away yet though," Fred explained. "We need to finish planning it with Baden and Bailey in the morning."

"OK. I'll be ready after breakfast – or during. Is this to do with Dimerie wines? Or disappearing people in Humber? Or Young Harry?"

"Yes, all of those," George nodded, and he yawned.

"OK, I'll go now. See you in morning." And he disappeared as suddenly as he'd arrived.

"Are we going to Dimerie or to Humber?" Fred asked.

"Good question," said George, yawning again, "but I think I'll have to leave it till we talk to the others to know what the answer is. Night night."

And so saying he turned over, leaving Fred to put out the glow and plunge the cubbyhole into darkness.

Fred lay thinking for a few minutes. Victor had made a good point – was it Dimerie wines, disappearing people or Young Harry? At the moment, it was Dimerie wines and Young Harry. Was it going to turn out to be disappearing people as well? How far would they have to travel? And his mind turned back to his mapping idea as he fell asleep.

* * *

The postbus emerged from the tunnel into the noonday sun and stopped under the shade of a large tree. Fred and George climbed off the top where they had been nestled amongst the bags and packages loaded up there, and stretched gratefully. It had not been the most comfortable way of travelling. Victor unhooked himself from some netting which covered the back of the bus where he had been stowed with some parcels in order to accommodate him and brushed the dust off his coat vigorously; there had been six travellers inside the bus, and two crammed onto the front seat beside the driver: if the boys had wanted to travel that day, those had been their options, take it or leave it. There had been far too many sacks of mail to be able to accommodate more passengers. Whatever Dimerie was lacking in wine it was making up for in correspondence, possibly from angry customers, Fred thought.

"How long do we wait here?" Fred asked the driver.

"As long as it takes to change horses and wait for the bus from Prancing Pony" was the reply as the driver unloaded some sacks from the top and moved them to the tree. "Don't go to the inn or we might not be here when you get back."

Fred wondered about the inn but found George had already checked.

"Apparently there's an inn about five minutes up the river," he said, "but it's not very big, mainly for people who want to go fishing, but it serves meals and has a couple of rooms. It's called The Bridge Inn."

They went down the track a little so they could see where their road led over a bridge which crossed a pretty river, with rushes and willows bordering it, and rushing water as it rippled over stones, and calm dark bits where it looked like fish might hide and catch unwary flies that came too close to the surface. A few yards upstream they could see a glint of white paint on a building, with letters on it that might have spelled out "Bridge Inn" had they been able to see all of it as it was partly hidden by willow trees.

"I wonder why it isn't right at the stopping point," Fred asked the others. "It would do good business."

"Think was here before tunnels," said Victor.

"Prancing Pony joins over there" and he pointed to a tunnel a little way off to the right from the way they'd come. His aim was emphasised by the emergence of another postbus, dust flying from its wheels as it drew sharply to a halt close to the other one.

They had established at a rushed early breakfast that as Victor had been to Dimerie as a kid, and had worked in the vineyards during the picking season a few years ago, he would be sufficient companion to save the Princelings from their own ignorance of the world. Posing as tourists would be the best plan for them. If they met Baden and Bailey in public they would appear not to know each other, although they had arranged to have regular get-togethers at places Baden had suggested. Their aim was to find out what had happened to the wine and why it had been kept such a secret.

Baden and Bailey would, of course, visit the House of Dimerie and expect a reception appropriate to official Buckmore visitors. Baden had warned everyone to be on their guard, not to go off on their own and always ensure someone else knew where they were. If anything happened which put them out of contact, the rendezvous point would be La Boucherie, an inn near the start of the tunnel where it emerged for Castle Fortune.

As they watched the transfer of packages and postbags from the newly arrived bus to their own, another carriage emerged from the Seventh Happiness tunnel, slowed as it went past the tree and steadied right down to negotiate the bridge. Fred, George and Victor watched as Baden and Bailey leant from their windows to look at the view, Baden pointing at the Bridge Inn upstream.

"I bet they had a nice breakfast," said Fred ruefully, as they had left to catch the postbus while Baden and Bailey settled to their second course.

"Just as nice. Slower," Victor said looking after them.

They returned to the bus where the driver set Victor on the seat beside him. Two travellers had gone over to the Bridge Inn, presumably for a fishing holiday. The number of packages and sacks had increased immensely, so the bus was still heavily laden. Fred was given the option of on top or at the back, and looking at Victor's face, opted to stay on top. More bags were then loaded into the netting at the back. The driver had a cursory look around to see whether anything had been forgotten, climbed aboard and they set off again.

After crossing the river they entered a tunnel once more, and after another hour or two emerged into a pretty wooded hillside. As the trees petered out they saw a dark castle in the folds of the meadows below them, and an inn to the other side with "La Boucherie" on a large notice at the side of the track.

The Princelings looked at each other and nodded.

"That must be Castle Fortune, then," said George.

They knew little about this land. Baden had given them a very quick summary – Castle Fortune had been virtually deserted for years since the last Princess had married into the Dimerie family, and there was no male heir. Dimerie used it for the wine cellars, but otherwise no-one went there. It was rumoured to be haunted. Dimerie had vast vineyards at Dimerie-Les-Landes which they would see as they arrived. They either crossed to Chateau Dimerie on a causeway, or bartered for a ferry, depending on the state of the tide when they arrived. George had a vague memory of a picture he'd seen of Dimerie at night with moonlight reflecting on the water behind it, so they gathered it was on an island of some sort.

They sped past Castle Fortune and on towards Dimerie. The sun was getting lower in the sky as they started to go through vineyards, and the smell of the sea filtered through to them even against the rush of air on the top of the coach. It was definitely not the most comfortable way to travel. Fred complained a couple of times but George reminded him of the very long walk from their own home to the Inn of the Seventh Happiness and how sore their feet had been afterwards.

"Well, it won't be my feet that are sore this time," Fred grumbled.

Eventually the bus arrived at a small town and pulled up on a stone paved area beside the sea.

"Dimerie! Dimerie!" called the driver as he got down, and was surrounded by officials and hangers on, all wanting post or packages or papers signed. The princelings clambered off the top and met Victor who was looking windswept and fly splattered from his full frontal exposure to the journey. The driver had had a visor and a coat to protect him.

Waves lapped at the edge of the jetty and they looked at them for a bit as they recovered their land legs.

"What do you think?" Fred said at last.

"How about that inn over there till the tide goes out?" said George.

"How about other inn for night?" said Victor. "Why go to Chateau straight away? Cheaper in les-Landes."

They followed the direction Victor had pointed, to the one a little way away from the bustle of the quayside. The town was busy, yet people seemed suspicious and they received wary glances from people as they passed. They entered the 'Bunch of Grapes', more appropriate for three tourists taking in the sights, and an air of tension enveloped them. It was as if everyone was waiting for something unwelcome to happen. They ordered drinks, asked about a room for three and sat down in one corner near to a very small fire that was struggling to survive.

There were five people in the room apart from the barman. They had looked at Fred, George and Victor when they arrived, listened to their transaction, and gone back to their drinks, with just a couple of them exchanging comments. Fred thought of the jollity in the Seventh Happiness and wished he might be back there very soon.

He went back to the bar.

"Do you have any food service this evening?" he asked politely.

"Aye," said the barman, handing him a food list, "But best order soon in case we close early."

"Why would you close early?"

"Well, we get weather and storms and emergencies like that. Both me and the chef would be on call for emergencies," said the barman, looking anywhere but at his customer.

Fred wasn't reassured. He took the list of food over to the others.

"It's a bit odd here, don't you think?" he said in an undertone as they made their choices.

After ordering, he came back with a second round of drinks and they discussed the barman's attitude.

They added it to the list of puzzles and helped their throats recover from the dust on the journey. The barman brought their food over and hovered over them for a moment.

"In the unlikely event there is an emergency," he said as if he reciting by heart, "you should stay in your rooms, under the beds or in a cupboard, unless you hear people shout 'Fire!' If you hear that, follow the corridor to one or other end and jump out the window." He turned and left them looking at each other in puzzled astonishment.

Dusk had settled over the town but they took a walk round the town to stretch their legs. A good strong wind sent clouds scudding across the sky but it was a pleasantly warm evening. It was just right for sailing, although they could see neither boats nor ships on the sea. The causeway was just about visible as a line of choppy waves breaking over something, and Victor said it would probably be dry enough to walk on in about two hours. They agreed staying overnight was a better idea than going across in the dark.

They stopped at the other inn, the Anchor. To their surprise, they were the only people inside and the barman looked strangely at them as they ordered their drinks. After discussing whether everyone had already taken a ferry across to the chateau, and wondering whether they could go and look at the vineyards tomorrow as a suitable thing tourists do, they finished their drinks and left. It was very curious that the expected hospitality of Dimerie, even on the mainland side, was so much less than they had been led to believe. They wandered back to their room and settled down for an early night. They may not have done much during the day, but travelling was a wearisome business. Fred and George shared a creaky double bed and Victor had a fold-down mattress which was perfectly comfortable, so he said.

Their muddled dreams were shattered by the sounds of running feet, breaking glass and shouts piercing the darkness. In their sleepy state they had just thought they should hide under the bed and in the cupboard, as had been suggested, when the door burst open and the room was filled with large people carrying swords and guns and smelling extremely smelly. They were lifted off their beds, their heads were stuffed into sacks or something else, and despite their struggles they were carried bodily out of the inn over their assailants' shoulders. As they kicked and yelled, their captors just laughed. Finally they were knocked on the head and they knew no more.

Chapter 3: The Golden Guinea and the Mare Swine

In which Fred and George find their sea legs, and Victor has to walk the plank

George realised he was coming to his senses when his stomach complained bitterly at being lurched around and his head complained bitterly at having been knocked about. He checked his other senses and found the nose was complaining bitterly about the smell of unwashed bodies, damp socks, marsh mud and centuries-old poo, his touch suggested he was free to move but partly wrapped in some sort of material which was swaying about, his mouth tasted dry with a sort of bitterness and saltiness about it, and he could hear creaking noises, slapping noises which echoed through the room where he was, rushing noises and the murmur of people above him, with occasional louder noises like orders being given. He decided not to open his eyes for a little longer, partly in case it hurt his head, and partly in case he could listen a bit more and work out what to do before anyone might notice he was no longer asleep.

As he lay there he worked out he was in a boat or ship, lying in something called a hammock that he had seen in pictures but never been in before – a stretch of material strung up at both ends so someone could lie between them comfortably and move with the motion of a ship without being thrown onto the floor. The murmur was probably the ship's crew, orders were, well, orders, creaking was the boat and the rigging and the sail, the slapping was the water outside the boat, as he was inside it and possibly below water level (which got him slightly worried). The rushing noises were also the water going past the boat. He wondered where Fred and Victor were, but he could hear no sounds of anyone else in the vicinity so he cautiously opened his eyes.

He gave himself full marks for his interpretation of the sounds. The room was dark with streaks of light slipping through the ceiling from above. He could see seven other lumps strung up in hammocks and he hoped Fred and Victor were among them. He tried moving slightly and stretching his legs and promptly fell out of the hammock onto a very hard floor, covered in slime and rubbish. It was disgusting and it stuck to his coat. Someone in the corner laughed at him.

"Awake at last are you? Can't take a sea bed?"

The owner of the voice and laugh was virtually invisible in the darkness and George had to look carefully to see him shuffling over to him as he was completely black. George thought of asking 'where am I?' and 'who are you?' but decided they were rather stupid things to say and he would find out more by watching and listening. Just then two more of the hammocks deposited their occupants on the floor with a thump followed by cries and groans and exclamations expressing dissatisfaction with the situation. The black guy laughed again and told them to keep quiet if they knew what was good for them.

"Where am I?" said one.

"Who are you?" asked the other.

"You've kidnapped me!" said the first, "You can't do that! I demand to see my solicitor!" he finished in a very haughty voice.

The black guy just laughed again and went over to the other five hammocks and poked the occupants. Judging from the wriggles that resulted – two of which led to further thumps as they fell onto the floor – the occupants were alive and kicking. He carried on to the end of the cabin and picked up a bucket which he threw in the general direction of the hammocks. All were now empty and the occupants picked themselves up, rubbing various parts of their anatomies, and sat around looking at the black guy and each other, blinking in the dim light.

"Right, you lubbers!" said the black guy. "My name's Frankie and if you know what's good for you you'll listen hard, work hard and keep your mouths shut."

He passed round eight bits of stale biscuit and a bucket of fairly clean water and a scoop. They each took a drink, and some of them nibbled the biscuit. George found his stomach settled down a bit, and tried to see whether Fred and Victor were among the party in the darkness. He rather thought they weren't and frowned. The haughty guy refused the biscuit saying it was disgusting and one of the other guys took it off him and wolfed it down.

Frankie waited for them to recover their senses a bit more then started talking again.

"You are now aboard the Golden Guinea, the prettiest barque that ever sailed the seven seas. You will do as you are told, you will work hard, and if you don't, you will walk the plank. That means you will find yourself swimming, possibly in shark infested waters, a thousand miles from the nearest land. You won't last long." And he laughed again. It was not a pleasant laugh.

"In a few minutes," he began again, "you will go up on deck and be allocated your duties. Have any of you been on a ship before?"

Most shook their heads or mumbled 'no' but the haughty one said "Of course I have, my father has a 40ft Solero yacht on the Humble; I've been cruising since childhood!"

Frankie chuckled. "Well, you'll know all about ropework then Mister. You'll be right at home!" and he chuckled again, sounding as if he relished a comic spectacle about to happen. He cut further chat short with "Right then, this way," and he took them to the foot of a ladder which he made them climb up, the first one pushing aside a hatch to let in sky and sea breezes and fresh air. They clambered up one behind the other till the eight of them stood in a gaggle on the deck.

To George's untutored eye it looked extremely pretty and extremely disorganised both at the same time. There were sails flapping a little in the wind above them, but mainly they were filled with wind and he started wondering what sort of forces the wind produced to propel them through the water. There seemed to be piles of ropes and barrels and nets and cages of chickens and baskets of fruit and vegetables propped up all round the place, although some did look as if they were roped together. There were about fifteen men up at the front of the ship, some more up the masts and tending to the sails, and a couple near the back, where a large person with a funny hat stood next to a small person with a handkerchief tied round his head who was tending a large wheel.

The hat person was looking over the eight of them as if they were cattle in a sale pen.

"Stay here and don't move an inch!" ordered Frankie. Looking around the ship, there wasn't much point in making a run for it, George thought, as there was no land in sight. They must have all thought the same as they all stood still. Frankie went over to the hat person, where they had a brief chat, looking back at the eight of them. Frankie nodded occasionally and then touched his hand to his eyebrow as he left the hat person and came back to the group.

"You two, join that group for'ard," he said pushing two small guys with white faces up to the main group at the front of the ship. "You, up the rigging and join the party on the mainsail." And he pushed two lean guys to the side of the ship where rope ladders stretched high into the sky leading to the knot of sails about halfway up the mast. They started climbing, looking fearful. "Hold tight and don't look down," he added, encouraging them, and they gulped, held tight and looked up to where three other guys looked down at them and called encouragement. "You two, go below down that hatch there - the men there will sort you out."

He turned to George and the haughty one. "You can go below and join the cabin detail," he said to the haughty one, "and you will come with me," he said to George.

He walked back up to the hat person and George followed, wondering why he had been singled out for this treatment.

"Cap'n Starling!" was all Frankie said as they reached him, and Cap'n Starling turned and looked George over carefully. Frankie left them.

"Sir," George said, thinking it might be a good idea.

"Mmm," said the Captain. "You'll do. Know anything about navi-ga-tion?"

"Um, only in theory sir," George said, trying to remember what he'd read about star navigation, azimuths, compasses and currents. Castle Marsh was close enough to the sea for him to have taken a mild interest at one point, but he had given up and moved on to other things when he had thought the chances of them leaving the Castle had been minimal.

"That'll do, that'll do. Pippin here will teach you. You're our new mascot. Keep clean, look tidy, you never know when... Carry on, Pippin," he said to the person on the wheel and he turned and left the deck.

* * *

Fred gazed out over the ocean, the wind whipping through his hair and lifting his ears like wings. He didn't mind the huge amount of swaying that accompanied his high perch, in fact he found it infinitely more comfortable than the journey on top of the postbus and a lot more comfortable than the short swaying and yawing they experienced below decks on the ship. The job of lookout, high up in the crow's nest, suited his personality entirely, and had it not been for the fact that he didn't know when, or if, it would end, he would have said this was the best possible thing to be doing on his holiday.

For two days now Fred had been a pirate, or at least an unwilling sea-going assistant, having been press-ganged by the pirates of the Meerschweinchen, as the ship was called, although everyone called it the Mare Swine. Victor had been allocated to the Quartermaster and was busy working out how to keep the captain and crew happy on very little in the way of vegetables and a lot of boring dried food. They had woken up in a huddle in the corner of a cabin with three others, including one of those who had been on the postbus with them. The first evening Victor had hissed at him that Young Harry was in the next working group to his as he had served out the 'stew'. They had managed to sit together after the meal, and quietly compare notes. Young Harry had had no opportunity to get ashore even when a raiding party was on, partly because they were still within reach of Dimerie. Now they had gone further afield, and as Fred gazed over the ocean, seeing neither ship, nor obstacle in the water, which were the main things he had been told to raise a warning of, he wondered what would happen when they finally reached their destination.

Young Harry had told him they had been stocking up the holds with wine and other produce from Dimerie and other castles on the coast. As far as he could tell, as he had not actually got onto the island before he was press-ganged, Chateau Dimerie had been held to ransom over their wine; the first stocks at Les-Landes had been taken some time ago, then the Chateau had been raided and not only wine taken but one of the princesses kidnapped and held hostage so Dimerie wouldn't call for help. Then the secure stocks at Castle Fortune had been discovered and at some stage the pirates were going to venture inland for those. Harry was hoping to settle in and gain enough trust to be able to escape when they went there. He had also reassured Fred when he couldn't find George, and told him as far as he knew there were only the two pirates operating together, their own Captain McGraw and Captain Starling. George must have been in the group that were sent aboard the Golden Guinea, Starling's ship.

Fred had been relieved to hear George had not met with an accident, but worried he was on his own in another ship. Harry thought they were going up the coast a bit, but the Mare Swine was bound for a southern country where they would trade the wine for gold, or whatever it was pirates wanted these days.

Fred took another special long look around him from the crow's nest. The black line of land on his left was still there, no bigger, no smaller, which was as he had been told it should be. He was good at looking out and Thinking at the same time, as he had a special watchfulness that had kept him and George out of trouble many times at Castle Marsh. He enjoyed watching the wind in the sails and it made him Think about his wind experiments, and he watched to see what he could guess of the wind's movement from the way the sail moved.

Suddenly one of the sails moved a bit to the left and he caught a glimpse of something in the distance just to the right of the bow of the ship. He waited till the sway of the boat gave him a second view, then yelled "Sail Ahoy!" as loud as he could down to the people on the deck below. A fairly garbled response reached him, which he interpreted by pointing and yelling back "Two points off the starboard bow" which he hoped was right, and if not, it would get them looking forward, anyway. If it was the port bow he could always say it had moved, he thought. He watched the sail grow larger, and remembered to look around in case anything else was happening. Apart from a few more birds following the ship, nothing else had changed.

One of the regular pirates came up the rigging towards him and squeezed into the crow's nest.

"Squeeze up, but stay here," said Rum, a smart looking red-headed guy with a black eye patch who had been very helpful to Fred. He looked at the sail, then looked all around just as Fred had done. "Good work, mate," he said and then slid down the rigging all the way to the deck, never putting a finger out of place. Fred could see him reporting to the captain, a big guy with black hair, eye patch, and a white z-shaped scar on his side. The men called him 'Feathers' when they were referring to him in private, although Fred hadn't worked out why. Fred thought he reminded him of someone he'd met recently, but knew it couldn't be the same person, so had put it out of his mind.

The ship continued to make progress towards the other one, and the land on their left started to get closer as well. Fred wondered whether he should draw their attention to it but decided not, as it had been there the whole time really. Finally they were within hailing distance of the other ship, which turned out to be a local vessel looking to escort them into the harbour, so they turned and followed it into the harbour of Porto Verde, where they moored at the quay just as the sun set and the wind was turned off.

Fred came down from the crow's nest and joined Harry and Victor helping to unload the wine. He did have a pang of conscience that he should be saving this wine for his friends back home, but he didn't see what else he could do really. He went back on board and drank some water, having got rather thirsty up in the hot sun all day. Suddenly he became aware of a lot of commotion on deck, and someone shouting "Clap him in irons! I'll see to him later!" He popped his head up out of the hatch just in time to see Victor being dragged away, his hands and feet chained together, and thrown down through the forward hatch. As he leapt from his own hatchway Harry caught hold of him and hissed "Leave it! We'll deal with it later!" and he stopped still, trembling with a combination of fear and anger, and wondering what Victor had done to merit this treatment.

Harry went and joined a party of people who were detailed to go in the small boats and row, dragging the ship out into the harbour away from the quayside, so they could no longer go ashore easily. Fred watched and wondered whether he should be doing something. Rum came up behind him.

"Your friend, the grey and white one," he said. Fred looked at him.

"He in big trouble mate. Tried to tell on us he did. Harbourmaster listened, then gave him back to us. Harbourmaster likes us too much!"

Fred looked worried, as well he might be. "Big Trouble" was not what they needed right now. He had to make sure Harry, Victor and himself all got back to their own land in one piece as soon as they could.

"What will happen to him?" Fred asked.

"Walk the plank like as not, when we're out in deep ocean," Rum replied.

Fred gulped. He felt responsible for Victor in some way. He didn't have long to work out what to do, and he hadn't got the faintest idea how to save him.

Chapter 4: Shipwrecked

In which George plots his course and Fred goes flying

Fred clung on to the crow's-nest for dear life. He had completely changed his view of this activity as a pleasant way to spend one's holiday. Around him the thunder rolled, the lightning crashed, the seas heaved and his stomach heaved with them. Every few minutes the ship lurched to the top of the wave where he plucked up the courage to put his nose out of the crow's-nest and look to see if there was any danger, and there was a momentary feeling of weightlessness before the ship rolled over the crest of the wave and down onto the other side, sometimes with a sickening crash that made Fred wonder whether the timbers could possibly stand the strain. Most of the rest of the journey through the trough in the waves, Fred crouched down, wedging his body in the little wooden basket and hanging on, not daring to trust the strapping Rum had kindly tied around him before leaving him to his shift. He wondered how long this watch would last as he couldn't see even Rum coming up to relieve him; surely no-one would try shinning up the rigging in these conditions.

The storm had come on swiftly after they had left the security of the harbour at first light. Despite grumblings from the more experienced crew the Captain had refused to return to its shelter and they had ploughed on, firstly through rough seas and strong winds, then through huge breakers, wind and rain, and finally through a full tempest with all its accompanying drama. They had hardly any sail up, just enough to give them a modicum of control, and most of the crew were below decks feeling horribly sick. The one consolation, thought Fred, in his few moments when he could think of anything other than survival, was that Victor had not yet been made to walk the plank, as no-one could keep a plank steady for long enough. Also, the Captain had wanted a decent supper (before the storm took full hold), so Victor had been let out of the brig to cook it for him. Indeed, the quality of his cooking was such that he might expect an indefinite stay of execution.

The storm had been raging now for over 24 hours, and Fred thought Rum's prediction it would be over in twelve had been vastly optimistic. He had no idea where they were, he had no visibility like he had on the journey down, and even when they were at the crest of a wave he could only see rain and storm clouds and choppy water. He was beginning to think the storm was lessening a bit, though it was getting towards nightfall, and there was no increase in the light, yet Fred was convinced the clouds were getting a bit thinner.

He poked his nose above the top of his shelter once more, took a look around, trying not to get salt water spray in his eyes, saw nothing, and hunkered down once more in his misery.

**

After three days of sailing, George was getting used to life on board the vessel. He enjoyed learning navigation skills from Pippin and making suggestions on how to allow for the combined effect of tide and leeway as the ship was blown through the water.

On the first evening they had arrived at a small fishing port where they had taken on fresh food and water, and all the new recruits had been sent below decks with Frankie to make sure there were no attempts to jump ship.

George had got talking to the haughty guy, whose name was Arthur, and one of the others, a nice guy with buff coloured hair who reminded him a bit of Fred, who was called Theo. Arthur was a princeling from Humber who had been sent on a similar errand to find out what had happened to the Dimerie wine supply. From the way he described it, Castle Humber was a very strict place where protocol was important. The king there sounded rather like George viewed his own king at Marsh; liked power, liked things just so, and liked the traditions observed with strict obedience to all rules and regulations. He could see why Arthur was so haughty, and wondered why he and Fred had not gained the same airs and graces. Probably because they weren't as close to the line of succession as Arthur, he thought.

Theo was completely different. He had journeyed on the normal bus from Wold and saw Arthur at some rest stops on the way. Arthur's carriage had turned back having deposited him at the Prancing Pony, so he had taken the post bus from there to Dimerie as the carriage could not be spared for him longer. Theo had met Arthur on the postbus, and they had compared notes on the wine situation on their way down to Dimerie. Theo had never been outside his castle before so it was a huge responsibility and adventure for him, and he had been glad to meet Arthur, who appeared so much more knowledgeable. They had arrived at Dimerie-les-Landes the day before George and Fred, and journeyed to the vineyards to ask about supplies, rather than go to Dimerie itself. They had stayed at the Anchor, which Theo described enthusiastically as 'great' and Arthur described as 'disgusting'. They hadn't found out much at the vineyards, though, except they didn't have any problem with disease and the harvest had been much as normal. They had been told to enquire at the Chateau and that was that, although they had been treated kindly, taken on a tour of the winery and been invited to take afternoon tea, so hadn't returned to the Anchor until nearly bedtime.

From George's conversation with the pair of them, he would have said Arthur had not much more experience than Theo, just a lot higher opinion of himself and of Humber's importance. As George stood at the wheel on the second day he had pondered the different castles and the way the kings (or barons, or princes) influenced not only what went on, but the way it happened. He also tried to work out who was next in the line of succession at Marsh – he and Fred hadn't taken much interest in family affairs, but now he began to think they should have done.

George kept quiet about his suspicions they were on their way to Humber, possibly to raid the castle of any riches a pirate might think worthwhile. It would hardly help Arthur or Theo to know. He wondered what he should do. He also wondered whether he would be required to take action in a raid. He couldn't see himself fighting or stealing, it was all entirely against his way of thinking. How would Captain Starling ensure his new recruits actually carried out these activities, or would they be left below decks once more and only the real pirates go marauding? An idea occurred to him. Once he had gained skill in navigation, and people trusted his course finding, would it be possible for him to deliberately scupper the pirates' plans by running them aground?

On the third day, George was at the wheel pondering this idea once more when there was a sighting of a ship from the crow's-nest above. They altered course to intercept the ship.

"All hands action stations!" called the Captain, and the regular pirates rushed to various positions including a group that went below decks and got ready some cannons which pointed out of the side of the ship above the waterline. The newcomers to the crew were pushed below decks except two that were sent up the rigging, and George who was still at the wheel. Pippin was at the masthead where he had run up a neutral flag as soon as the ship had been sighted.

"Ahoy there, what ship?" called Frankie, standing beside the Captain.

"The Angry Bittern, out of Dun" came the reply from the ship, which turned out to be a fishing vessel. It was returning to port after a short trip as there were forecasts of major storms due in the next 24 hours, and they weren't taking any chances. It was heading for its home port of Dun, which sounded familiar to George, although he had no idea why, and the Captain asked Pippin and George to devise a new course to take them to a bay or neutral harbour with shelter from a nor'wester.

Pippin pointed on the chart to a huge estuary with a narrow entrance a little further up the coast, so they set a course and estimated how the tide might run in order to help them get into the sheltered lake formed by the confluence of many rivers joining just before they flowed out to the sea through a narrow neck.

The rest of the evening was spent working their way up to the entrance as the wind was against them, but by turning one way then the other they arrived at the right place on the incoming tide and rode it through a low cliff-lined passageway which then broadened out into a huge area of brackish lagoons and waterways and reeds, with a long seawall stretching far inland along the north side. George continued to find things were familiar to him, especially that seawall. He rather thought he should try and get to it if he possibly could.

They moored in the shelter of some reeds and put out extra storm anchors, and the captain gave orders for a general clean up and mending session, so people were put to work on mending sails and dressing ropes and making the ship ship-shape during the night, before dawn broke and the first signs of the storm started whistling through the rigging. And there they stayed for the next two days while the storm raged about them.

***

Fred had a vague feeling the quality of the waves had changed and they were giving a choppier, but also more surfing like sensation as if they didn't have as much depth to them and were spilling out over a smooth base. He stuck his nose out once more and could see nothing in the near-darkness. Rum had still not been up to relieve him from his watch, and he was cold, wet, miserable, and nearly exhausted.

The wind may have been a little less, but there was still thunder in the area, long rumbling noises passing from cloud to cloud as if they wanted to keep the pirates surrounded.

Suddenly there was a loud cracking noise and the mast in front of Fred disappeared, falling with its sails crashing into the sea and the rigging, still attached, pulling the ship sideways after it. The ship pulled round and the waves crashed against its side, tipping it right over, then pulling it right back again. Fred shut his eyes and hung on tightly as he seemed to almost lie on the waves on the first sway, then whiz back over and lie on the other side as it came back again. It started to return the other way as the waves broke over the ship again, and the crow's-nest sheared off the mast like a matchstick snapping in two. Fred was flung into the air with it, finally being plunged into the waves and going down, down, before it started to rise up again, breaking the surface and bobbing upright like a cork. Fred coughed and spluttered and start to scrabble to untie himself, then stopped as he realised the crow's-nest was floating, so despite being soaked, he might as well stay strapped to it as it could keep him alive.

Despite his desperate situation, after over 40 hours just clinging to the shelter of his crows-nest and being thrown around the sky in it, Fred fell asleep.

He awoke with the realisation something was strange, and the strangeness was that he was still. He was lying, strapped to two bits of wood, on a sandy and gravelly shore, and he had sand in his mouth which he spat out as best he could. He rather thought he needed some fresh water. He sat up and wriggled out of the straps holding the wood to his body, and thanked the two planks for keeping him afloat, wondering what had happened to the rest of his crow's-nest and indeed to the rest of the ship. He thought of Young Harry and Victor with a momentary lurch of his heart, but decided he wasn't yet safe and needed to sort himself out, then look carefully for signs of the ship and its inhabitants.

He got to his feet, a little wobbly, and stretched a little. He didn't seem too badly off, a little sore, a few bruises, but nothing broken. His hair was a mess so he spent a few minutes brushing himself off, which made him feel better and more able to face whatever happened next, the first thing of which was to assess his situation.

The beach stretched away from him in two directions. In the third was the sea, looking pale grey-brown and choppy, but the wind had died and the storm was over. It was probably early to mid morning, Fred thought, judging by the quality of the light. The fourth direction was a large sandy hill, with pockets of long marram grass at the base giving way to different types of grass as it went up. It was a sand dune, and with any luck there was more grass-covered sand dune behind it. Fred struggled up the slope till he was standing on top. He found the sand dune went along the back of the beach like a huge sea wall, stretching as far as he could see. Beyond, it dropped down to a nice lumpy turf area with more dune-mounds here and there, then there was a thin line of scrub and a few trees, then it gave way to marsh. And from his vantage point on top of the dune, Fred's excellent eyesight could see far over the whispering reeds. There in the distance, glinting in the sun as it filtered through breaks in the cloud, were the spires and towers of a castle standing on a rock in the middle of the marsh.

Chapter 5: Castle Marsh

In which Fred meets two members of royalty and George gains three companions

"Harrumph," snorted Uncle Vlad, as Fred finished his story. "You seem to have been meddling things way beyond your competence, my lad!" he said sternly.

Fred hesitated. "Well," he said finally, plucking up courage to contradict his uncle, "I think I have learned a lot and in any case things have turned out well enough. And I have made good friends and learned much about the ways of the world," he added, feeling he really had to press his point home, mindful of something either Baden or Prince Lupin had said before he left Buckmore. He felt a momentary pang as he realised he hadn't thought of Baden for days.

"And George is on the verge of an important discovery which will be of great use to society. Prince Lupin is sponsoring him in this venture."

"Harrumph," said Uncle Vlad again, "Prince Lupin, well, he's just playing games that one." He muttered this under his breath but perfectly audibly to Fred. Fred wondered once again if there was something Lupin, Nimrod and Baden had kept from them, but felt he trusted them rather more, if anything, than he trusted his Uncle right now.

Something had been going on at Castle Marsh while they had been away, Fred was sure of it. He arrived after a three hour trek over the marsh, finding some of the regular tracks had disappeared and so having to retrace his steps and find alternative routes. He and George had wandered extensively, exploring the marsh and its ways, and he was fairly sure he entered the marsh near Summernot, which was only an hour or so at a jog. He scaled the northeast cliff of the castle as they usually did, as he and George had found a way up long ago, making small adjustments here and there to make it perfectly suited for their methods. It was rarely guarded, even so Fred moved cautiously, to make sure he regained his place in the castle without being seen. Once inside he returned to the cubbyhole adjoining Uncle Vlad's apartments from where he and George had left for their earlier adventure through the tunnel that had appeared. The tunnel was still there, the cubbyhole had not been used, and its entrance was still well concealed from prying eyes. He visited a number of their favourite areas, in order to re-establish some sort of pattern to his movement, as if he had just been out of sight for a few months, rather than not actually there at all, then he went back to Uncle Vlad's quarters and knocked on his door.

The person that opened the door was not Uncle Vlad, nor his butler cum secretary, FGP. No-one knew what FGP's real name was, it was lost in the mists of time, but his initials were generally given other descriptions, including Few Good Parsnips, Five Gold Puddings, and even Fred's Grand Parent, which was almost certainly not true. The person that opened it was a female, a very beautiful female, who looked Fred up and down and said "Yes?" in a polite but confident manner, and made Fred completely reassess his mission.

He introduced himself and learnt her name was Kira, and he got into conversation by explaining he'd been on holiday and had only just heard she was here. "Have you been here long?" he enquired, and followed it up with asking what she thought of Castle Marsh.

"It is very isolated," she said. "Not like my home at all, even though that is on an island," and they went on to discuss the differences, people she had met here, whether it would be appropriate to have dinner together later, and where Uncle Vlad's apartments were now. "Oh, they are still here really," she said,

"But he is mostly in the Regency during the day, and just comes back in the evening to see that I am well, then goes off to his formal quarters in the South Tower."

Fred was puzzled by all this, but it forewarned him to take care when he went to the 'Regency', by which he took her to mean the Registry, which was where all the king's business was conducted. As far as he knew, Vlad had never used quarters in the South Tower, which was where the king and the crown prince lived. Was Vlad now the crown prince? Had the king died and the crown prince assumed the throne? He hadn't seen the crown prince since he was small, when he had tried to bully Fred and George although he wasn't much older than them. He was a small dark haired chap, as he remembered.

Uncle Vlad harrumphed again and Fred came back to the present. "What do you want to do now then?" he asked, eyeing Fred closely.

"Well, we have a problem. There are pirates sailing up and down the coastline, planning raids on Castles and trading valuable things with other coasts. George and some other friends are missing and I think we should find and rescue them. And we also need to free those that are imprisoned in Chateau Dimerie, and free the hostage they have taken so that Dimerie can once more trade its wines with the rest of the country," Fred finished.

"Good statement," acknowledged Uncle Vlad. He turned away and went over to a window to stand and look out for a moment. Fred watched him and thought of what he might do if he could get Vlad to help him.

"Where is the captain of the ship that was wrecked, do you know?" asked Vlad.

Fred shook his head. "I was thrown clear before the ship foundered, if it did, and I expect it did," he said. "The wreckage could be anywhere along the coast, and survivors could equally be anywhere."

"Well, you're not wrong there, young Fred," came a voice from a tapestry behind Fred, which was pushed aside and Captain McGraw of the Mare Swine stepped forward, followed by Rum and another chap. "Bow, nephew, before I sort you out once and for all."

Fred looked at Vlad, who had turned around and was looking at him with a strange smile on his face. "As I said, my dearest nephew," Vlad said sadly, "You are meddling in things way beyond your competence. You already know more than you should."

"But who are you?" asked Fred of the Pirate Captain, astonished.

"I am the Pirate King," said Captain McGraw, and Rum and his mate behind him said; "He is, Hurrah for the Pirate King."

"It is a wonderful thing, to be a Pirate King, but I am also, rather inconveniently, officially king of Castle Marsh as my father died two months ago. So as there was no-one else of the blood left, because I have been, er, persuading them to leave over the last few years, I appointed our dear Uncle as Regent. Now you turn up, and your infernal twin George is still around too, I hear."

Fred stood silent for a minute, trying to reconcile this large person with the z-shaped scar with the young person he and George played with when they were very small. He had a feeling he was going to need an escape route very quickly and he wished he was rather closer to Uncle Vlad's old apartments than the Regency. He hadn't been here much when it was still called the Registry, and he was desperately trying to remember a short cut or secret passage in the vicinity. He was going to have to be very lucky, he thought. He wondered where the tapestry led, as Ludo (which was the Crown Prince's given name) had come through it with the other two, and they couldn't have been just hiding behind it. The three of them had moved over to Vlad by the window.

"So, your Majesty," said Vlad to the Pirate King, King Ludo of Castle Marsh. "We need to restore the trade in Dimerie's wines to save an uprising of all the castles in the land, and we need to warn Starling he has a tricky customer in his crew."

"We also need to work out what to do with the

increasing number of hostages we have at the Chateau. It is really most inconvenient of people to send official envoys there." King Ludo responded with a sigh. "How is our guest?" he added.

"Oh, she's fine," replied Vlad. "She's got my quarters, and she understands she's here as an envoy, so she's not worried at all. She's as quiet as a mouse. I've got a couple of my girls keeping her company too."

Fred edged back slightly towards the tapestry. The others continued to talk about what they should do. Just then a knock came at the door and FGP poked his head round.

"Beg pardon my lord, oh, your majesty," he added, and bowed to King Ludo, "There's a party at the gate asking for sanctuary. They seem to be led by one of your nephews."

Fred's heart leapt as he realised it must be George, but his feet leapt at his chance and he slid through the tapestry as the attention was away from him.

As luck would have it, the passage behind the tapestry emerged in the reception hall in the wall behind a suit of armour. Fred saw George and three others looking at the portraits hanging on the wall, and he could hear George pointing out the steam machine in the background of the one of Prince James.

"Psst!" he said, and George turned and grinned as he saw him. "Over here, quick! Danger!"

George grabbed Theo and said to the others: "Quick" and they ran over to Fred.

"We need a quick way to our tunnel in Uncle Vlad's apartment," Fred said to George and as George thought, a slab of stone swung back in the plinth of the suit of armour. "Go!" said Fred, stuffing everyone in, and they fell over each other as Fred pushed and jumped in after them, swinging the door shut behind him.

They untangled themselves from the heap they'd fallen in, George muttered "You've done it again Fred", and then led the way along the tunnel that had opened up in front of them. In just a few minutes they emerged in their cubbyhole, coming out of the back of the fireplace in Vlad's (or now Kira's) apartment. The four of them squeezed into the apartment and George did the introductions.

"Theo, Arthur, Sundance, this is my brother Fred," said George.

"Pleased to meet you. Listen, we need to make a plan," said Fred.

"Just what is going on?" asked Arthur in his haughty voice, which Fred didn't like but if George had taken up with him he must be ok, he reckoned.

"We also need to act fast, I don't think we can wait here to discuss it," continued Fred. A thought suddenly occurred to him. "Look, we need to go down the tunnel over there, get ourselves out of the castle, and then we can sit and discuss it."

The others nodded obligingly.

"George, you take them down there, go for five minutes then wait for me. If I don't catch you up in another five, get yourselves to Buckmore as fast as possible. Oh, and the Pirate King is our new King here," he added, and he slipped out of the door and along the corridor, hoping they would act speedily on his command.

George looked at the others, as surprised and bewildered as they were, but pointed at the tunnel in the corner and told them to go down. Theo led the way, followed by Sundance, an agile-looking brown haired guy with a white scar running from his ear to his forehead, ruining his looks. Arthur hesitated, so George pushed him, and he fell headlong down the tunnel, landing in a heap for the second time in almost as many minutes.

There was only one way from the tunnel in their cubbyhole, and George knew it was hours before they would leave the damp earth of the tunnel under the marsh, reach a zigzag, and then a division in the tunnel. After five minutes, as Fred had ordered, they stopped, and started chatting quietly. Arthur had at last gathered some sense of urgency and adapted to the situation he had found himself in.

"So what is going on here?" he asked plaintively. "You said we'd be safe here, be able to get help."

George nodded, realised that wasn't much help in the darkness, so said 'yes' out loud.

"I'm guessing," he continued, "That Fred arrived here by some other route, found out that the Pirate King who is behind all of this is something to do with our castle, and he's just escaped from him."

There was not much in the way of comment to be made about this, but Theo wanted a bit of clarification.

"So you haven't got a safe haven here after all. And Castle Marsh is manned by pirates?" he asked.

"Something like that. We'll wait five minutes as Fred asked, then we'll have a very long walk to safety and real help. How are you guys?" he asked.

Tired, thirsty and hungry, seemed to be the general consensus, and as George knew that already, it just helped them to know that he knew and wasn't asking them to do things without considering their situation.

They had already had a narrow and difficult escape from the Golden Guinea. George had worked out during the storm where, roughly, he was relative to his home, Castle Marsh, and planned to shin out on one of the anchor chains at dead of night and swim through the channel to the seawall. It wasn't going to be easy as the channels could get choked with reeds very easily. The trouble was, the four of them had been locked in one part of the ship, so without bringing them into the plan, George was not going to succeed. It took them both nights of the storm to break through the wood around the lock to free themselves, then they followed Sundance to the bow of the ship and slid down the chain. They nearly roused the watch, Frankie, as Arthur insisted they ought to go off the stern as it was lower in the water, but Sundance pointed out the bow was head to wind and closer to the shore. If they went that way they'd be under cover of the reeds more quickly.

Then, just as they splashed into the water, well, three slid silently and one splashed, a shout came from the ship and there were sounds of running feet and a lot of splashes as if people were diving in. Torches were lit and guns were fired into the water. The four of them were terrified but George just hissed at them to keep going and not look back. As they reached the comparatively dry land underneath the seawall, they recalled that the torches had been held near the side and rear of the boat, and the shots hadn't been fired in their direction, and they concluded that someone else had chosen the same moment to run for it.

"If we'd gone over the stern of the boat we'd have been done for," Sundance had commented. George was grateful he hadn't had to say it, and hoped Arthur would learn from the experience.

They had run along the sea wall, keeping a low profile so as not to be seen in the growing light, then come down off the wall and started the long journey through the marsh. George had warned them it could take six hours and would be physically hard, as they were continually clambering down and across water filled ditches, then up the other side, until they finally reached the large marsh and George could use some of their old trails. These had surprised him as they seemed remarkably well maintained, not the old water-deer trails he and Fred had used in the past. But apart from keeping a careful eye out for trouble, they had said nothing and kept going till they reached the castle gates.

Now, they had received a cautious welcome at the gate, waited in reception, and been bundled by Fred into a secret tunnel, then bundled by George into a second secret tunnel. They wanted to know what was going on, and so did George, he said.

"We'll have to wait till Fred catches up with us to find out, though," he told them.

Five minutes were nearly up when they could hear the patter of little feet approaching them from the direction of the castle. There was more than one person coming, and George felt a little alarmed. Had someone found their secret tunnel?

"Are you there?" called a voice in the darkness softly.

"Yes, Fred," answered George equally softly.

The brothers greeted each other with a hug, partly as it enabled them to locate each other in the darkness, and George judged by the perfume of the stranger that Fred had brought a female along.

"Who have you brought with you?" he asked.

"Brother George, may I introduce Princess Kira of Dimerie," Fred replied and although no-one could see her, they could feel that she smiled as she received the introduction.

"But how did you know my full title, Fred?" she asked.

"I Thought about it," Fred replied. "But now we must set off, we have a long way to go."

Chapter 6: The Best Laid Plans

In which Fred and George find something nasty near the woodshed

The Inn of the Seventh Happiness was a welcome sight for five weary travellers as they rode in on a simple wagon that had been sent back for them. Theo and Sundance had drawn the short straw to run all the way and charter it for them, Sundance had driven it back for Fred, George, Arthur and Kira, while Theo had made appropriate arrangements at the inn with the landlord, Argon, who was anxious to hear from Fred and George himself.

Despite the extra transport they hadn't arrived until midday. They were soon settled in three rooms, Princess Kira being given the guest suite, Fred,

George and Arthur sharing the second room in it, and Theo and Sundance sharing the servants' room. George told them it was still much larger than the cubbyhole he and Fred usually received, so not to be aggrieved at their status.

Near the zigzag in the tunnel they had debated long and hard about which route to take. The Inn was hours away, but was a known quantity and was a hub of information and options for help. The other tunnel was a complete unknown. It was not even known whether it did lead anywhere, let alone where. Consequently the next step was to get to the Inn and make further plans. Now they were settled and had eaten and drunk their fill, they gathered in the guest suite to continue the debate about their next course.

Fred and George were of the opinion that Prince Lupin should be involved; however they were also worried about Baden and Bailey, who must be imprisoned in the Chateau along with numerous other messengers. However as Kira pointed out, the Chateau was a comfortable place to be imprisoned, there was plenty of food and company, and if the Pirate King was based at Marsh they were unlikely to be in any immediate danger. She herself, she added, had hardly felt in danger as a hostage, it was more like an extended duty visit to another castle. She had rather hoped she was not under scrutiny as King Ludo's next bride, but she supposed he was better than some kings she had heard of. Fred wanted to ask whether she had heard of Prince Lupin of

Buckmore but felt strangely reluctant to talk of Lupin's qualities to her.

Arthur was keen to get word back to his father at Humber, but Fred and George were equally unwilling to let him do so. The regime at Humber did not sound as if it would produce a happy result. Theo didn't think the folks at Wold would run to the aid of Dimerie, although it would be useful for them to watch out for their own territory if they had warning.

"I don't think they would be likely to tackle Marsh without very good reason to," he said.

"What do you think, Sundance," Fred asked.

Sundance spoke slowly as if he was picking his words carefully: "I think sending word to Buckmore is wise, as action is needed and they are men of action. But we could go back to the Chateau ourselves, leaving Kira here in safety so she doesn't get kidnapped again, and free the prisoners. That would have more impact on the pirates," he finished.

"How do you think we could free the prisoners?" Fred asked.

Sundance said he had an idea, but didn't want to talk about it here. "Needs secrecy," he said, putting his finger to his lips.

George looked at him. "We don't really know anything about you," he said. "We met up in the

Golden Guinea, you helped us escape, you seem very self-sufficient and able to cope. I watched you about the ship and you knew what you were doing. You went ashore with the provisioning party although not on the raiding party. How do we know we can trust you?"

Sundance paused for a bit before he spoke. "You don't," he said, and he looked round them all one by one as if reading their faces. "And I don't know whether I can trust you. In the current circumstances I don't feel ready to. But I will go back to Dimerie with you and we will agree a plan, and we will carry it out as best we can. With me, you will stand a better chance of success than you will on your own."

"How did you get that scar?" asked Fred, waving in the general direction of Sundance's eye.

"I trusted someone against my better judgement," he said.

Fred looked at George. They could see they were in agreement.

"How dangerous do you think this mission will be?" George asked Sundance.

He pursed his lips and looked around at them again. "It is quite possible somebody will be injured, or possibly killed."

Most of them moved uneasily in their seats. George didn't fancy the being killed bit. Fred was suddenly reminded of the rest of the crew of the Mare Swine. If Ludo, Rum and the other guy had survived, how many others had? Where were they? Were they the only ones left? Had Harry and Victor escaped, swum ashore, or clung to wreckage long enough to be washed ashore? Were they already victims of this adventure? He had not been looking forward to telling Argon that Victor was lost, although Argon had just nodded.

"I was lost for a while," he had said. "I was found again. He'll come back."

Fred hoped he was right. He liked Victor and thought he was one of the best people he'd met on his travels.

Princess Kira spoke. "You mean to leave me behind for my safety, but do you really think I am safer here on my own than with you? The roads are not safe, you know."

Fred started to say something, but stopped. George took over. "I think we are worried for your safety, yes. You are also an important person in the political workings of this. But I would be happy to take you with us as you seem to be resourceful and, er, spunky."

Fred nodded, but looked worried.

"What do you think, Sundance?" George asked.

"It will be dangerous," Sundance replied, turning to

Kira, "You will need to do as you are told at times, when you would rather do something more exciting. You must not let these people risk their lives for you unnecessarily. Can you do that? Follow orders you don't like?"

"You wouldn't believe how often I have to do that," said Kira wryly, and they agreed the party would stay together.

***

The wagon stopped at a roadside shack by an large tree and they looked wistfully at the Bridge Inn a little further down the road.

"It does look nice," said Fred, comparing the idea of an inn for lunch with the dry sandwiches the shack offered.

"Well, could we go down and let the horses rest here while we have lunch?" suggested George. So they arranged for the horses to take a break in the field while they walked down to the inn, and sat on a bench in some uncharacteristically warm autumn sunshine watching the river, supping their drinks and eating a nice "Carrot-planter's Lunch".

"Would this be a good place to discuss our plans for when we get there?" Fred asked Sundance. "We've only covered generalities and possibilities so far and it's difficult to think when we're bouncing about in the wagon."

"How many people were inside?" Sundance asked as he hadn't gone in to order.

"Only four, all look like they're fishing – they've got long leggings on to keep them dry," Fred replied.

"OK then," Sundance said. "Who do we think is in the Chateau, and how much help might we get from them? Kira?"

"My father has a lot of people to run the household and three of my brothers are very keen on sport things, two are in the pentathlon competition team, so they shoot and fence. There are a team of twenty household security people. Most of the security people are on the mainland though, to ensure the wine is ok. I guess the pirates have taken care of them already though," she said sadly.

"How many visitors had been detained when you were moved from Dimerie to Marsh," he asked.

"I don't know, not many, I think."

Sundown looked at the others. "You know of envoys from Humber, Wold, Buckmore..." he said to the others.

"Not sure how many from Buckmore," George said, looking up. "Harry didn't get there, Baden and Bailey we assume did, don't know where the other messenger went."

"We have sent three envoys," said Arthur.

"Same here," said Theo.

"And none were on the ship like Harry?" asked Fred.

"Not on ours," said Theo. "I don't suppose you really found out as you were right up there most of the time." He was referring to Fred's time in the crow's-nest.

"No," Fred realised of course, no-one could tell who had been on the other ship.

"Well, we could assume we've got at least a dozen envoys, possibly lots more, depending on whether the other Castles have sent them. They will have to be imprisoned to get them under control. They can't possibly have hoodwinked them," said Sundance.

"Erm, we do have extensive dungeons, I'm afraid," said Kira, "although they are now used as wine stores."

"If they've cleared the wine out they'll have loads of room for these prisoners then," said George and Kira nodded.

"OK," said Sundance. "Now listen closely because I don't want to say this so that anyone can overhear."

And he bent his head and talked low and fast to them explaining the general plan for rescuing the envoys and liberating any wine left.

"The problem," he concluded, "is how to stop the pirates doing it all again."

Fred thought for a moment. "I don't think we have to worry about that ourselves once we free the envoys and get all the castles to know the situation. We have found out, embarrassingly, that our uncle-cousin, our home castle, is the source of the problem, so the castles can take more appropriate steps than we can."

Kira nodded. "And now we know about the pirates," she said, "We can all be on our guard against them."

Sundance straightened up. "Excellent," he said, "any questions about what you have to do?"

Everyone shook their heads, although Arthur looked like he was going to ask something and then changed his mind.

"OK then, let's get going again," said Sundance, and they all got up. Fred stopped.

"Just one thing," he said. "Can we stop at a place called 'La Boucherie' on the way down. It was where we agreed to meet Baden in an emergency, so we should check."

"That's good," said Sundance approvingly. "We'll do that, and the same will apply to us – this will be the place we rendezvous if we get split up."

**

They drew in at La Boucherie as the sun disappeared behind some thick clouds and it looked like it was going to rain.

"Just take a quick look," said Sundance, "I think we should press on."

Fred and George got out of the wagon and went into the restaurant. There was a funny smell in there they didn't like, and it was very quiet. They called out a few times, then decided to go and look in the kitchen. No-one was there, but there was a meal in preparation, or would have been a few days earlier... It was attracting flies and there was mould starting to grow on it, but otherwise it looked as if the chef had just been called away for a moment.

"I don't like this," said George, moving towards the back door.

"Neither do I," replied Fred, following him.

They went through the back door and George reversed straight into Fred and pushed him through the kitchen and into the front.

"Don't go there," he said urgently, "I don't think we'll be coming back here."

Suddenly there was a yell from outside and they rushed to the door. George spotted something on a notice board to one side and grabbed it as Fred opened the front door and started running to the wagon.

"Fred, George," yelled Sundance, turning the wagon so they could drive straight out of the restaurant onto the road.

Fred ran to the back of the wagon and jumped on, as the others leaned past him to try to catch hold of George and pull him aboard. Off in the distance they could see a horde of pirates coming up the road from Dimerie.

"We need to take cover!" shouted Arthur.

"Come on George," shouted Theo, leaning out of the wagon trying to catch George's arm.

George made a superhuman effort and leapt aboard clutching a piece of paper in his hand, as the wagon gathered speed and headed for the only other place of shelter they could see - Castle Fortune.

Chapter 7: Castle Fortune

In which George becomes a code-breaker and Fred asks plenty of questions

The gates of Castle Fortune lay broken at the side of the archway and a tangle of creepers threatened to grow over the entrance to produce a rather more impenetrable barrier. Fortunately, the wagon got through without any difficulty. Arthur and Theo jumped out as they passed and dragged branches, broken barrels, even the gates themselves to the entrance to build some sort of barrier to keep the pirates out for at least a few minutes. Sundance drew the wagon to a halt under an arch in an inner courtyard. Fred and George jumped down and, while Fred helped Kira, George looked round the nearest doors.

"This one leads down, possibly to the wine stores," he said, running on, "and this one leads into a long room, a guardroom maybe." He continued to call out what he thought the doors hid until he came to one which he disappeared inside for a few seconds, then stuck his head back out and called to the others, who were by now approaching his location, "this way, it looks like it could be useful."

They entered a small hallway with a staircase which wound up through the castle. They could see it went up four storeys before disappearing through a door in the wall.

"Yes," agreed Sundance, "this looks useful."

They sped up the stairs and ran through the door at the top, which had a lock on the inside and could be barred against anyone following them. They were in a long room with white plastered ceilings and brown arched beams, wooden panels on the walls to half way up when the plastered walls took over. There was a large fireplace at the far end.

"Did the pirates follow us in?" Sundance asked Theo and Arthur. They shook their heads as they caught their breath, neither being used to quite so much exercise. "Let's check those doors over there," continued Sundance, "and decide what we should do next."

The doors at the end, on either side of the fireplace, led into a long corridor on the left hand side and a small enclosed spiral wooden staircase on the right.

"I think that will lead to the gallery," said Kira, pointing upwards to a minstrel gallery running along the right hand side of the room just below the ceiling. "This must be a dining hall; we came up the servants' route." Most of them nodded, their own castles had similar arrangements.

"Well, we have a room with two entrances and exits, so as long as we aren't approached from both directions at once we should be ok," said Sundance, sitting down. "Everyone ok now?" he asked them, and they nodded and took their places around him. "Then let's work out what to do next. Is it still a good idea to go to Dimerie and how can we avoid the pirates if they are on the road?"

They all looked as though they were thinking, although Fred really looked as if he was Thinking, and Arthur didn't really look as if he knew how to think, but was quiet, anyway. George rubbed his shoulder and stretched it around a bit absentmindedly.

"Are you hurt?" asked Sundance with a frown.

"I think I must have pulled it a bit when I was trying to get onto the wagon. It's nothing." He rubbed it some more, and suddenly remembered he was holding a scrap of paper he'd taken from the inn.

"What's that?" Sundance asked.

"I saw it in the inn and grabbed it as we left. It said

'F+G' on it," George explained. He opened it up looked at it, then looked longer at it.

"Well?" asked Arthur.

"What does it say?" asked Sundance.

"It's in code," George said, and passed it round. They each looked at it, Arthur turning it upside down as well, before he handed it to the next person. Fred gave it back to George and looked at him expectantly. The note had read:

G+H; ibwf ftdbqfe Ejn. tfou C up M-C gps ifmo. Vjmm ijef bu G. ep opu sfuvso ifsf. Baden.

"How do we know what it says?" said Arthur in frustration.

"Give me a minute," said George, his forehead wrinkled as he puzzled it out. "Oh!"

Fred smiled, he'd been sure George would be able to solve it.

"It's from Baden," he said, looking at Sundance. "We trust him, we came with him from Buckmore. It was him we were looking to meet at La Boucherie."

"OK, what does it say?"

"Now, I think it's a simple code shift as it starts G +H, and it's F+G on the outside – F+G is obviously Fred and George, so he's addressed it to us. So...

h-a-v-e have, e-s-c-a-p-e-d"

"escaped" said Fred, looking over his shoulder.

"D-i-m"

"Dimerie. Have escaped Dimerie. Good," said Fred.

"s-e-n-t B t-o L-B" spelled out George.

"He's sent B – Bailey? To L-B, Prince Lupin at Buckmore - that would be a good thing to do – send for help."

"Also to advise what's going on at Dimerie... I hope this Bailey has made it," said Sundance, and the others nodded.

George continued "f-o-r h-e-l-p. Yes, for help. Next comes u-i-l-l h-i-d-e a-t F. Something 'hide at F'."

"He's miscoded it□ I think he means 'will hide at F'." Fred said, "Where's F? Next?"

"d-o n-o-t r-e-t-u-r-n h-e-r-e then Baden in clear," finished George.

"Do not return here. We shouldn't be here!" said Fred starting to get up.

"No, 'here' was the inn," said George catching hold of him, "rest, brother."

Sundance nodded. "Good work George. So there is some hope of a rescue party, but do we know when he left the note?"

George looked at it on both sides a couple of times. "No, he hasn't dated it," he said. "But it hasn't been rained on."

"Where's F?" repeated Fred, looking at the others.

"Fortune!" said Kira, "He came here."

They looked at each other. It was a big castle. Was Baden here, with anyone else he had escaped with? That would be good. "We'd better have a look around," said Fred, "We need to find him before we each think the other party are pirates."

"Good thinking, Fred," said Sundance. "I think we could split up into two parties for this. One go round at this level, the other go down to the cellars."

"How long do we look for?" asked Kira.

"Let's give it till sundown, then all come back here whether you've found them or not," Sundance said. "I'll go down with Arthur and Theo, you three do the upper levels."

They set out on their quests, Fred, George and Kira leaving through the door near the fireplace after the others had gone back down the stairs.

"What if they are between the ground level and this one?" asked Kira.

"I think we could cover that if we think we hear them," answered Fred, and they went quietly along the main passageway, turning corners cautiously, looking round before they moved into the open, and stopping every now and then to listen. Eventually they came round to what they thought must be the end of the castle at that level.

"Shall we go up here?" said George, pointing to a stair spiralling up inside a tower.

"Might as well," answered Fred, and they went forward, Kira following Fred, then George in the rear. The stair curved round the wall and occasionally there was a slit window where they looked out on the surrounding countryside. "We ought to watch for pirates as well," said Fred and they nodded in agreement.

They skipped one floor and went along the corridor on the next. It had a low ceiling and they thought they were probably pretty much on the top floor.

"Stand still," hissed George suddenly. They stood, and listened, but could hear nothing. Fred and Kira looked at George questioningly. He shrugged. "I thought I heard something."

They walked on but George stopped again and turned round. They all stopped, and George looked carefully behind them. "Swap over," he whispered to Fred, and they changed places so that George led on and Fred brought up the rear. They went a few more paces then Fred stopped and turned round. He looked carefully, then looked at George and nodded. He pointed to an archway a little further ahead, and they crept forward to it and stepped out of the corridor itself. Fred stood in front of Kira, but she looked over his shoulder, not wanting to miss anything. They could all hear a quiet shuffling noise now they had stopped.

Slowly the noise came closer.

"Is it a ghost?" Kira breathed in Fred's ear.

Fred shook his head, no, and said nothing. His heart was beating very fast. He didn't know whether it was scared of the shuffling noise or excited by Kira so close to him.

The shuffling noise went past them and then disappeared.

"Did you see that?" whispered George, puzzled.

"What?" responded Fred, equally quietly. "I didn't see anything, except it all went fuzzy for a moment."

"Exactly," whispered George. The brothers looked at each other, then at Kira.

"I couldn't see a thing," she breathed.

They cautiously looked out of their alcove. There seemed to be an obstruction in the corridor, but they couldn't make out what.

"It's beginning to get dark," Fred whispered, "We'd better get back to the others."

Their alcove seemed to have a set of narrow stairs in

the corner. They decided to go down two levels and hope to get back to their own hall rather more quickly that way. They seemed to be in quite a hurry to get down the stairs and they crowded up against each other until they got back to the hall they had started in. Once there they relaxed by the fireplace. The others were not yet back.

"Umm, did we see something odd upstairs?" asked Fred when they had sat there a bit.

"Er, yes, I think so," said George. "I don't know what it was, and I don't really want to find out."

Night had fallen, and they looked at the fireplace wishing it had a nice comforting fire in it.

"We really need a nice comforting fire," said Fred, wistfully.

A small glow appeared in the fireplace and grew to a small sized log fire, all of its own accord. Kira started shaking.

"What is it, Kira?" Fred asked, going over to her and putting his arm round her shoulders.

She pointed at the fireplace. "H-how d-did that get th-there," she stammered.

"Well, it's just something that's been happening to me lately at my home castle, and I just thought it was worth a try here," he said, squeezing her and rubbing her shoulders comfortingly.

"Good idea," said George. "How about saying we need to find Baden?"

"I don't think I'll push my luck," said Fred, grinning and letting Kira go. "I wonder where the others are?"

"You know we were doing this search till sundown and then coming back here?" he said after a while.

"Er, the others aren't back, are they?" said George, and they looked at each other in the dark room, their faces only visible in the light from the little log fire.

"Oh, dear," said Kira.

* * *

The day dawned grey and overcast through the window above the minstrels' gallery. The little log fire had kept going all night, which gave them comfort as every now and then they thought they heard something. Fred had said they'd take turns at watching, but in truth, those that weren't watching had hardly slept. Kira had taken her stint at watching too, and Fred had not wanted to leave her watching all alone but felt it best to let her, especially after the comment she had made about being used to doing things from duty.

They stretched and yawned and decided it was time to be officially awake. The fire seemed to brighten up, as if it might be needed, but they had no provisions. There had been some on the wagon they had brought with them, but they hadn't thought to bring any indoors with them in the hurry to avoid the pirates.

"Why didn't the pirates chase us in here?" asked Kira, as they discussed the lack of breakfast.

Fred shrugged. "Maybe they had something better to do."

"Maybe they heard it was haunted," George added, remembering the strange fuzzy experience of the evening before. They all shivered.

"I'm glad we had the fire," said Kira, gazing into it.

"We need a plan, Fred," said George.

Fred sighed. He couldn't think of what to do for the best, and he had Thought about it when he was on watch. They couldn't carry out the raid on Dimerie without the others, and as they seemed to have disappeared, he wasn't too keen on going down to the cellars to look for them. And was Baden still here or had he gone back to Buckmore – or even Dimerie?

"We either go down to the cellars and see if we can find anyone, or we run away, I think. I can't see too much point in just the three of us going to Dimerie. Running to Buckmore for more help would be my preference."

George nodded. "I know it doesn't sound very brave, but I think it is sensible. I'll do the cellars if you think it best, but I'm beginning to think I'm running out of bravery. It all seems very difficult to me."

"Oh, come on guys, show a bit of spunk," said Kira. "We have to rescue the others and then save the world you know."

The boys looked gloomy, then noticed her face and they burst into giggles. Kira joined in.

"That's more like it, guys. You got me worried then."

"I think we've just had a bit more of an adventure than we were planning, Kira," said George. "The pirate ship was scary, the storm was scary, the pirates are scary, and that's one big scar Sundance sports. I've never fought anyone in my life and we've all been going along with his plan. I'm just an engineer, not a fighter."

"And I'm just a Philosopher," added Fred. "And I don't like what's going on at Castle Marsh. But we need to settle your situation first. What do you want to do?"

"I suppose I should go home, but there's no point in doing so till it's safe. If the Prince of Castle Buckmore is sending help, then we'd better wait for it, but if we have lost Sundance and Theo and Arthur in the cellar, then surely we ought to find them?"

"Have you ever been to Buckmore?" asked Fred.

"No, but there was some talk of my sister Nerys going in a few weeks now, and I might have gone with her," replied Kira. "I hadn't been many places before I got taken to Castle Marsh."

"Have you been here before?" asked George.

Kira shook here head. "It was strictly out of bounds. The wine store, of course, but also, rumours it was haunted. Nobody would go to the cellars at night. My mother came from here though and she told me lots of stories about the castle."

"Anything that might help us find the people who went to the cellars?" asked Fred.

Kira thought for a moment. "Mother always used to giggle when she spoke about the rumours, and sometimes go off into a little refrain of 'Rumour it's haunted, haunted by Rumour' which I didn't understand but just seemed silly. I used to imagine Rumour was a person she knew who was still here."

"Well, I think we are going to have to go and look aren't we," said George with a sigh. "How long shall we put it off?"

"Oh, I suppose we'd better go now," said Fred.

And so saying the three of them got up and went down the back stairs. Down to the entrance hall.

Down again to a basement that looked like it had been the castle kitchens. And down once more into a low, vaulted warren of tunnels where occasional shafts of light let some glimmer onto the shadowy alcoves where once Dimerie's wine had been stored, but now there were just dust and cobwebs.

Chapter 8: All Washed Up

In which Victor and Young Harry have an adventure all of their own

Victor gazed up at the sky and wondered where he was. He coughed a bit and spat a bit as his mouth was full of salt and sand. He moved each leg gingerly as if experimenting, and decided he was all there, and mostly in one piece. There was a lot of aching and his ribs felt as if he had been in the big washing tub they used at the inn for all the guest bed-linen, and then through the mangle used to squeeze all of the water out of it when it was done. He sat up and looked around him.

There was some sea, and a lot of sandy mud, or muddy sand. He decided he wouldn't test it too much to find out which. There was a rock shelf stretching out into the sea and lots of birds pecking in the mud and water beside it, and some perching on top of it too. There was a low cliff behind him with lots of steps in it, not steps that were cut, he decided, more like shelves of harder rock that had withstood being worn away by the sea. It looked much the same in each direction, but it did look as if there might be some sort of activity to his left a long way off, as birds were flying about as if there were some fish to attract their attention. He stood up, brushed himself off, and set off in that direction.

"Arrgghh."

Victor stopped as he heard the sound. He had only been going for about ten minutes and the birds were very much closer. He reckoned another ten minutes and he would be there. He looked around but couldn't see where the sound had come from.

"Arrgghh," it came again.

This time Victor could see a large animal with hardly any arms or legs, dressed in a smart silvery grey coat with spots on. He thought it might be something called a seal, which he had heard of but never seen before.

"Arrgghh," said the seal.

"And arrgghh to you too," said Victor, discovering his voice was very husky and his throat parched. He hoped there might be some fresh water he could drink when he got to the birds or, better still, a nice bottle of Vex beer.

He went on a bit and started to notice more bits on the beach. He moved down the slope slightly and discovered loads of things had been washed up to the waterline in the storm. Apart from things from ships, and there were plenty of those, there were fishing nets, oranges, seaweed, bones, bits of wood, and a funny lumpy thing almost the same size as him. He kicked at it a bit with his toe.

"Arrgghh," it said.

Victor jumped back in case the seal attacked him, then he wondered why the seal was wrapped up in a damp and soggy cloak. The cloak and its contents moved. He looked over it, ready to run at a moment's notice.

"Arff, I feel awful," came a voice, as cracked and husky as his own, but familiar all the same.

"Harry?" he asked, cautiously.

"Who's there, where am I?" Harry asked, still muffled in his cloak.

"It's Victor," he said, and helped him untangle himself from the heavy material.

"Victor, thank goodness it's you," said Harry, emerging from the folds. "Where are we? What happened?"

"The ship sank. I don't know where we are. There may be something up there. Where the birds are flying about," Victor replied. "I was walking there and I saw you. I wonder if anyone else survived?" and his mind went to Fred and the other people who had been press-ganged like themselves.

"What shall we do?" asked Harry plaintively, still clearly suffering from disorientation, and Victor thought he had probably had an almighty bang on the head and might be concussed.

"I'm walking that way. See if we can get help. Do you want to come too? Shall I come back for you?"

"No, I'll come with you." Harry replied, "I don't want to be left alone and I feel awful."

"OK," said Victor, helping him up. "Can you walk? Do you need a stick?" and he gestured to the spars of ships, bleached driftwood and even whole tree trunks littering the shoreline.

Harry tried his feet out. "I can walk," he said, staggering a bit but looking determined.

So they set off along the beach again.

As Victor hoped, the birds were indeed flying around hoping for some fish from a small boat beached by the storm. The owners were still unloading what they could salvage from it, but clearly it had fared better than the Mare Swine as it was mostly in one piece. They hardly stopped as

Victor and Harry came towards them, but nodded and responded kindly when Victor asked them about a town or inn in the area. They learned they were near to Castle Wash and King Lynn was friendly to shipwrecked sailors as long as they weren't pirates.

"Oh, no, not pirates." Victor and Harry had chorused, meaning they weren't, and learned a number of pirates had been washed ashore, or trapped in the mud by the outgoing tide, and what was more, there was tell of a pirate ship run aground a few miles out in the mud flats waiting for the next high tide to float it off.

"If you can help, get along to see King Lynn straight away," said the older of the two people, and he pointed them in the direction of Castle Wash.

"Do you think this is a good idea?" asked Harry after a bit.

"We must help," replied Victor. "We may need theirs."

Harry nodded, that made sense, he thought. He didn't much feel like thinking though. And nodding was a bad idea.

They came round a low headland and could see Castle Wash ahead of them, perched on the edge of a wide river where it entered the broad expanse of the estuary, or inlet; it was such a large area Victor wasn't sure whether it was classed as estuary.

"Shall we be helpers, or should we try an audience with the king?" asked Victor.

Harry groaned. "I don't know," he said, clearly still worse for wear.

"I shall use your status as official messenger for Buckmore," said Victor. "And talk official language," he added.

Talking official language was something Victor had previously done only in the presence of Prince Lupin and a few other prestigious visitors to the Inn. It gained them not only an audience with the king, but a full run-down of the situation of the stranded pirate ship, The Golden Guinea. The king seemed almost gleeful he had the opportunity to get Captain Starling clapped in irons and strung up to the gallows, and they gathered the castles on this stretch of coast had suffered severe predation from the pirates over the last few months. Urgent action was needed, to row out to the ship before the tide reached its height, as they reckoned the ship would probably float within one hour of high tide. The current would be against the shore party, so more manpower was a great bonus, especially as a Buckmore representative, however ill, would be able to bring extra kudos and weight to the proceedings.

Victor and Harry joined a large number of people on the quays of the river as it ran past the castle walls, preparing boats and weapons. They settled themselves into a party led by the king's steward, a brown haired guy called Monty, and set to with a will when the boats were launched into the stream.

It was tiring, rowing, and they were not at their freshest, despite the refreshment given to them in the king's hostelry. However within half an hour they had got close enough to the ship to see figures bustling about the deck, and four small cannons peering out of the port side. The rowing parties swung around to the starboard side and when Victor next looked, he could see the ship was leaning so much they couldn't get the cannon holes open, so they were not going to be fired upon unless the tide came in and lifted the ship.

"Come on men," called Monty. "We have to reach them before the tide lifts the ship upright." And they rowed even harder.

As they got close, things began to rain down on them, pots, boots, bailing hooks, buckets. The pirates were throwing things in an effort to drive them away.

"Good news, men," called Monty, "they've got no spears or weapons to throw. Listen up now, as we pull alongside, ship your oars in neat order, run to the stern here, pick up a sword and run up the netting as quickly as ever you can. Don't push and don't fall over yourselves in the rush!"

And that was exactly what happened. Another boat had thrown netting up the side and had got up it before the pirates had managed to disentangle it and cut it away, and the boarding parties swarmed over the side and engaged the pirates. There seemed to be surprisingly few of them and they were soon overwhelmed. Victor did a lot of running around waving a sword, but neither struck out at anyone nor was he attacked by anyone, so he looked valiant without being in any danger of harming either a pirate or himself. Harry had a cursory sword fight with a small person with a handkerchief tied round his head, but he surrendered after a couple of parries, possibly just as exhausted as Harry was himself.

Monty received the sword of an overpowered Captain Starling, clapped him in irons and delivered him down to the boat. The pirates were put to the oars to do most of the rowing on the way back, but the tide was with them now, and they got back in less than a quarter of the time it had taken them to get there.

There was a great deal of jollity in the castle that evening, and a good meal with plenty of drink was set before all those who had taken part in the capture of the pirate vessel. Harry was feeling much better and Victor was feeling like he'd not had such fun for a long time, especially since he was being waited on, rather than running around serving everyone. As the evening drew on, a messenger came for them asking them to attend the king in his chambers.

They, along with a few people from other castles that

had joined in the attack, were led in by Monty and were welcomed by the king who praised their bravery and their part in the adventure.

Harry bowed and murmured things like "it was nothing" while Victor thought it was jolly good and they deserved all the praise that came their way! But he bowed politely too, and listened to what was said next.

"I have decided," said the king, "to interview Captain Starling and offer him a choice of abandoning piracy or swinging from the gallows. I dislike capital punishment, but sometimes one has to be firm. I felt it important," he continued, "to have you here, as representatives of other castles, and especially one with the influence of Castle Buckmore."

Many of the others looked over at them, and while Harry just stood proudly, Victor felt a little nervous of being included in such an elite band.

They all stepped back to make a gangway as Captain Starling was brought forward to stand in front of the king.

"Well, Starling," started the king.

"*Captain* Starling, if you don't mind, your honour, your graciousness," interrupted Captain Starling, waving his manacled wrists around.

"Hmm," said the king. "You have been making a nuisance of yourself along this coast for far too long.

Many people have suffered because of you, let alone trade and provisions. What have you to say for yourself?"

"Your majesty, I am, how shall you say, indebted for the way you have given me a chance to speak," Starling started, swaying around and looking at all the people in the room as if he might find someone who could save him. "I am just a humble soul driven to making a living on the high seas when all my loved ones departed. I fell in with a bad crowd, and," he added, turning back to the king, "was forced against my will to carry out acts that led to the ruination of people who had worked hard all their lives, just so another could make his pieces of gold."

"And who might that be?" asked the king.

"Why, your honour, most respected and beloved king. None other than King Ludo of Castle Marsh, masquerading as Captain Feathers McGraw," said Starling.

A gasp rippled round the room, although this was clearly not news to all those present.

"Yes, we had heard of the vagabond king," said King Lynn. "Many are the princelings driven from Castle Marsh in order to allow him to maintain his dastardly lifestyle. Only two we know are still alive, still maintain their claim to the bloodline and we know not whether they are still there."

"I know nothing of the bloodline, my lord, my most noble king," squirmed Starling.

"Well, Starling," the king began, and those close heard the captive mutter "Captain" under his breath, "it seems you shall have an opportunity to earn my clemency. What can I offer you that will stop you returning to your old ways if I free you?"

"Oh most glorious king, all I long for is a tall ship and a star to steer her by," said Starling, gazing at the ceiling and holding his wrists forward in supplication.

"Hmph," said the king. "And then you will carry on your old ways on some other shore, no doubt." He looked at Starling sternly. "I shall give you a commission," he said. "If you carry out this commission and return, I shall give you a small amount of gold and freedom to settle wherever you wish. If you do not return, I never want to clap eyes on you again. Is that clear?"

"Yes, most worthy and admirable king," said Starling, although there seemed to be a false note in his voice.

"You are hereby commissioned to sail west in your ship the Golden Guinea, and open up a trade route for bananas. I have heard they are grown on small islands in a place called the Caribbean. Have you heard of it?"

"Oh yes, most worthy king," said Starling, and now

he looked quite interested, as if going to find bananas was the thing he most wanted in the whole world. "Um, if I'm going to go straight for this commission thingy, do you think I ought to change my name?"

"If you wish," said the king. "Let my steward know the name by which you will be known but now leave, and do not come back, unless it is with a guaranteed trade in bananas."

So saying the king waved at his steward and the pirate was led away, presumably to settle on a new name and return to his ship, with his crew, paltry as it was.

The king stood, and withdrew to his chambers, and the rest of the party dispersed. An assistant to the steward, named Mike, came over to them.

"Would you like to go to your quarters now?" he asked, to which they agreed, and Mike led them to a small room with a little sitting room attached. "The steward would like to speak to you as soon as he has finished the king's business," he said. "Would you mind waiting up for him? He shouldn't be long."

They nodded and relaxed with some more refreshments that had been thoughtfully placed in a large fruit bowl on the table in front of the window.

"What did you make of Captain Starling, then?" asked Harry.

"He was odd. Even with the people I meet." Victor

replied bluntly.

"What's this about the king of Castle Marsh, though? Didn't Fred come from Castle Marsh?"

Victor nodded. "Sounds bad," he said. "Can't imagine Fred or George being caught up in it. They were captives too, weren't they? Fred, anyway. They didn't know about pirates. Going to Dimcrie to find out about wine," he added.

They nodded at each other and said nothing else, lost in their own thoughts. These were not profound, to be true, as tiredness was only an inch away.

A knock came on the door which prevented them from nodding off, and they stood up as Monty entered.

"Sit, sit," he said. "You must be exhausted after your adventures." They nodded and slumped back in their seats.

"A few of the guys from Humber are keen to be getting down to Dimerie and sorting out any remaining pirates," Monty said. "King Lynn is very keen to trap King Ludo aka Feathers McGraw and bring him to justice. What do you think?"

Victor and Harry both nodded, Harry adding "Buckmore would want justice."

"I thought as much," said Monty. "By your leave, I have already despatched a summary to King Lupin, although I did call him Prince as he prefers. My king is a stickler for titles," he added. "I hope you don't mind my usurping your role as messenger," he said to Harry, who shook his head. "I have suggested he might send reinforcements to meet us at Castle Dimerie, or a suitable rendezvous in that area, to see if we can round up the pirates once and for all."

"Sounds good to me," said Harry. "Shall we stay here till we receive an answer, or shall we move on and prepare the way?"

"I'm glad you suggested that," said Monty. "It was part of the debate that perhaps we should send someone back to Dimerie to gather the latest intelligence. You know at least some of the pirates by sight, I presume."

"Only the ones on our ship, and as that foundered I doubt whether those ones are back at Dimerie, more likely to be between here and Humber," Harry said, and thought some more.

"We could do with going back to Dimerie, though," he said, "even if only to free the people at the chateau. There must be a large number and there was talk of a hostage having been taken."

"Good," said Monty. "I think you should rest here tomorrow, then the next day start out for Dimerie. With any luck you might be able to pick up the scent before it goes cold."

"How do we know Captain McGraw wasn't shipwrecked up this coast?" asked Harry.

"We assume he was," said Monty. "But he has an extraordinary knack of finding his way out of sticky situations. He is one of those people that appears to have nine lives. I'll leave you now. Have a good rest and I'll speak to you again in the morning. Ignore any dining bells, I'll give word that you are to have something sent up for breakfast, however late in the morning."

They expressed their thanks to him and Monty left them for the night.

"What do you think of it all, Victor?" asked Harry.

"How do they know there are lots of pirates left at Dimerie?" asked Victor.

Harry looked at him. "I don't know," he said.

They exchanged worried looks. Almost telepathically they decided to sleep on it, getting up, finding their beds and falling asleep as soon as their heads hit the pillows.

Chapter 9: Dungeons and Rumours

In which Fred and George rescue an old friend and a riddle is solved

Fred, George and Kira crept along the dim vault, brushing cobwebs away as they passed. They could hear a low moaning and occasional whispering noises. Fred's heart was beating fast again, and as Kira was in front of both of them, he thought it was more to do with fear than anything else. He thought he should not be more afraid than Kira, but then again, he didn't see any reason why not. They moved closer to the sounds, which seemed to be coming from behind a cellar door with bars on a small window in it. Kira stopped.

"That looks like one of the dungeons, and the door is closed," she whispered.

"Maybe the ghost is trapped inside," said Fred.

"Don't ghosts go through walls and things?" asked George.

They moved forward again, and stood on tiptoe to look through the window.

"Aaah!" came a number of screams and groans from within.

They stepped back, not being able to see anything.

"Who's there?" asked Fred in a firm voice.

There was a scrabbling from within as if people were getting up and falling over and pushing and shoving. A pale face appeared at the window.

"You're not the ghost!" said a mousy haired chap, who immediately disappeared sideways to be replaced by Arthur, who was also immediately replaced by Sundance.

"Good work, chaps," he said. "Can you get us out of here?"

George was already looking over the outside of the door.

"There is a lock, but I can't see a key. Hang on a minute."

He tried the handle and pulled. The door swung open.

"It wasn't locked," he said.

"No handle on this side," said Sundance, checking, "it would have been horribly embarrassing if we had not been locked in all this time.

"Who was the other chap?" asked Fred, referring to the sandy haired guy.

"Oh, he's one of the others who were here when we came down. We came in to see to them and got shut in ourselves by the ghost," Sundance explained. "Can you get a light from somewhere? A couple are injured and I want to see whether we can move them."

They looked around but Kira was already looking in a cupboard and brought out both a torch and a tinderbox to light it. She brought it back, glowing nicely.

"I think one person should stay outside at all times," said George as they all started to go inside to look.

"Well, I've been trained in first aid," said Kira, "so I need to go in. Do you want to stay here on guard, and maybe one or two of the others as well?"

George nodded and Sundance pushed Arthur and Theo out of the dungeon to stand guard with him. Fred and Kira went inside.

As dungeons go, it was quite comfortable. It wasn't wet or dripping slimy water down the walls, there were no rats, there was old hay on the floor and some benches to sit on. There was a small water-pump in one corner and two buckets, one of which looked clean, and the other, placed over a small hole in the ground, which didn't.

On one of the benches lay a person with his head wrapped in a dark coloured cloth, and next to him sat another, nursing an arm. The sitting one said hello, and waved Kira over to the one lying down.

"I haven't been able to do anything as we couldn't see to do it," explained Sundance. "I guessed by feel he had a head injury, but I don't know more."

"Hello, I've come to help you," said Kira to the injured person. "I'm just going to wipe your head with some clean water to see what's wrong."

"I don't think it's much," said the injured person in a croaky voice. "It hurt like hell to start and I thought I might have cracked it, but today feels much better. I can't open my eyes though."

Kira gently sponged his face and head with the water and some cleanish cloth she had picked up in the cupboard.

"It's a nasty slashing wound," she said, "but it seems to have started to heal, although you'll have a huge scar, I'm afraid." She carried on bathing his face. "Your left eye might be affected by the swelling around the wound, I think. The right one is just covered in blood, I think once I get it washed. How's that?"

And as she finished the injured person opened one eye.

"Phew," he said, "that's a huge relief. I really didn't want to be blind. Silly thing really, didn't see the pirate hidden in the gateway as we ran in. Who are you?"

"I'm Princess Kira of Dimerie," she said.

"Oh, really?" said the person. "I'm Baden, steward to Prince Lupin of Buckmore, and I am so pleased to meet you! You were the hostage, weren't you? Who..." and he would have asked who had rescued her but Fred, overjoyed to see him, pushed past and shook him by the hand.

"Baden, fantastic! Oh, well, no, sorry about your head," he said as he saw what a mess Baden looked.

"It probably looks worse than it is, Fred," Kira said soothingly. "Head wounds always bleed a lot."

"Glad to see you, Fred, that's great, we can have a chinwag, work out what's happening then plan what to do." Baden brightened up and sounded much better. "But first I think we'd better leave before the ghost comes back."

"Is there really a ghost?" Fred asked.

Arthur heard him and moaned in fear, while Sundance just said, "well, something pretty much like one, anyway."

"Let's go back to our room upstairs, that seemed safe," Fred said, and he led the way with Kira, followed by Sundance, Arthur, two strangers (one of whom had a broken arm or shoulder that Kira fixed into a sling for the time being) and Baden who was supported on either side by Theo and George.

They paused at the entrance hall.

"I don't suppose that wagon is in sight is it?" asked Fred, going over to the door cautiously.

"Why?" asked Sundance.

"It occurred to me that we left some provisions on it, and if they are still there we could do with them."

They looked at each other, told Kira to lead the others up the stairs, then both slid outside into the damp and drizzly day. Fred slid round the courtyard in one direction while Sundance went the other way. Naturally the wagon was right at the farthest side from them. It was quiet in the courtyard, with an occasional pigeon flying from the roof to make them jump, but they could hear no other sounds. They reached the wagon without incident.

"Watch the gate while I unload some useful stuff," said Sundance, who had packed the wagon in the first place. Fred watched the gate until Sundance gave him some packages to carry, then they both went back, each taking their own route, till they reached the entrance hall again.

"No sign of anyone then," said Fred.

"May be too early for them," said Sundance, and they took the packages upstairs.

They found Kira paying more attention to the two injured people, and Arthur standing by her saying his hand hurt. George looked at Fred and Sundance and shrugged expressively. They unwrapped some dry food and some fruit, which had survived the journey very well, and a sack of carrots, which they handed round. Everyone tucked in with a will.

"Do you realise we haven't eaten for three days," said Baden, sucking the juice from the apple.

"What happened?" asked George, so Baden filled them in on events at Chateau Dimerie.

He and Bailey had arrived in the afternoon just before the tide came over the causeway, so crossed hurriedly and been admitted to the Chateau as the official envoy from Buckmore. They were well received, although there was an air of tension, and Princess Nerys, who was helping her father as he seemed somewhat feeble, explained that the failure of the crop and letting down all their customers had a devastating effect on them all. She had shown them to their rooms after a small meal and left them. In the middle of the night Baden heard strange noises and, looking out, saw ships at the town across the water, heard screaming and running feet, and saw people being thrown into the ships like baggage.

"That sounds like us being press-ganged," said Fred.

When morning came they couldn't get out of the rooms, they were locked in. Eventually someone came and dragged them out of their rooms down to a cellar where they joined six others who were imprisoned there. There was food, water and they were occasionally visited by guards who seemed to be pirates. They could hear noises further down the corridor their room opened onto, and discovered more envoys that had been imprisoned there. They reckoned there were about thirteen more people in addition to the eight of them. There they stayed getting very bored and frustrated till one morning when Princess Nerys was pushed into their cell with them.

"Oh, no," said Kira. "Was she all right?"

"Yes," said Baden, "although she had challenged the pirates and told them off for making her father ill, so they decided she was also a troublemaker and had to be confined to teach her a lesson. This was good for us," he continued, " as we got the whole story from her, found out about you being taken hostage, and that you were no longer at the chateau – where did you go by the way?"

"Castle Marsh," she said, grimly.

"Oh, so we were right, it was Marsh under that pirate get-up," said the sandy-haired guy, who turned out to be Princeling Lance from Humber.

That night the storm blew up, and Baden started working on a plan. Next evening when the guards came with food, Princess Nerys acted ill, to draw them in, and Baden, Bailey, Lance and the others made a break for it. Princess Nerys agreed she would take her chance at getting out of the room, as she did not want to leave the chateau while her father was still there.

The plan worked well, they got up to the cliff level, and the group split into two, Baden, Bailey, Dougall (the one with the broken arm) and Lance went down the cliff on the seaward side and threw themselves into a boat rocking about at the bottom. Luckily the storm was abating and they were able to make the boat stay afloat and steer towards land. They avoided Les Landes, and headed inland, reaching La Boucherie just about breakfast time, as they had to keep hiding whenever they thought they saw something, and keep to the land rather than the road. At La Boucherie they had had a nice breakfast, discussed the possibility of lunch with the owner, who was going to fix them up something special, and then they scouted around for a bit.

"We decided there were too many pirates, or just general ne'er-do-wells, even if they aren't connected with the pirates, to risk staying at La Boucherie, and we also felt we needed help, so I sent Bailey back to Buckmore with a detailed message." Baden continued. "I wanted to be on hand in case something happened to Princess Nerys, so we agreed I'd come to Castle Fortune and investigate the state of the cellars, never thinking the rumours of it being haunted might be true."

He put his hand to his head a bit and Kira passed him more water.

"We had a bit of a fight just after we left La Boucherie. I left you a message."

"We got it," said George. "We got chased away by pirates though."

"Yes, there seem to be a lot of vagabonds in this land. Where do they all come from?" asked Baden rhetorically, although Kira answered.

"When my grandfather Fortune died, a lot of the villages around had no-one to give their allegiance to. Grandfather Dimerie offered land-holding, but people refused, saying they wanted to farm, not grow vines. Then we had people who arrived just because life was good here, then it started not to be so good. We had enough trouble protecting our vines and not enough care was given to the people. That's what my father felt anyway, and he tried to improve things once Grandfather died, but it was too late I think."

Baden nodded. "You are probably right, Princess. Well, we arrived in the early afternoon, had a good look around, and surprised some more vagabonds or pirates who were sifting through some old chests in a store-room. We had a fight and I got slashed, Dougall got his arm done in, and we retreated to the vault as the safest place to hide. We were wrong! That evening there were a lot of strange noises and we got a bit scared, I'm afraid. We backed into the cellar, and suddenly the door slammed and the light went out and we were trapped. I think I was bleeding rather a lot and my head hurt, and I reckon I passed out for a long time. The others were worried anyway."

They nodded.

"Did you see the ghost?" asked George.

"Only a general impression of something white and fuzzy," Baden replied.

"It's been back a few times, looking in," said Dougall. "You can hear it shuffling down the steps.

Brought us food though, a couple of times."

"That's odd behaviour for a ghost," remarked Fred, looking at George in a puzzled way. They all fell silent for a while.

"No," murmured Kira quietly, and they looked at her.

"Sorry," she said, "I just meant, no, it couldn't be."

"Couldn't be what, your highness?" prompted Baden.

She laughed. "I only thought ... My mother used to sing this jingle, I told Fred and George last night." She smiled sadly. "'Haunted by Rumour'. What if Rumour is a person? He'd be very old by now, and shuffling about is about all he could do."

"Have you ever heard of a person called Rumour?" asked Fred.

"Well, yes," Kira replied, "but I've only just remembered. It was the name of my grandfather's retainer. There was always an assistant from the family Rumour that looked after the kings of Castle Fortune."

"And is that who we saw upstairs yesterday?" asked George.

"Probably," Kira said. "How silly of me. Why didn't we just say hallo and talk to him?"

"I think you acted wisely, your highness," said Baden. "If he's been living here alone all this time, he may not be entirely sane."

Sundance walked over to the window and looked out.

"I think we may not have been entirely sane to have listened for so long without posting a look-out," he said. "There appear to be hundreds of armed people surrounding the castle."

Chapter 10: The Battle

In which Fred and George are overwhelmed by events

The overnight bus from the Prancing Pony stopped suddenly as it emerged from the tunnel into the wooded hillside above Castle Fortune. Victor fell onto the floor inside, Harry rolled backwards into the seat as he had been facing backwards. Princeling Hunston of Wash braced himself against the window but slid sideways all the same, and Princeling Merlin of Humber did the same on the other side of the bus. The pannier of food they had brought with them sat safely on the seat next to Harry where it had been thoughtfully strapped in when they left.

"What is it, highwaymen?" asked Harry, moving to the window. Hunston put a hand on his arm, cautioning him not to pull back the cover too quickly. They peered out from under it, to see a person holding a weapon across his arm talking to the driver in low tones. They couldn't make out what they were saying except for occasional words like 'pirates' and 'Dimerie' and Hunston thought he heard 'help', 'Vexstein' and 'Buckmore'.

"I hope so," said Harry, as he reported this back to the others, "Buckmore should send aid here, but surely the messages from King Lynn will only be received today."

"Maybe he has received other intelligence," replied Hunston, "Vexstein too. That guy looks as if he knows what he's doing with that weapon." He pulled his head back inside and sat back and gestured for Harry to do the same. Merlin and Victor looked at them, back in their seats where they belonged.

"It looks like we may be among friends. Let's just wait for a bit." Hunston said to them. "Shall we have a spot of breakfast while we wait?"

They had just started on a packet of breakfast biscuit when there was a knock on the door and it opened. The driver was outside, the armed person standing behind him.

"Sorry for the emergency stop," said the driver. "It seems like Vexstein and Buckmore have taken things in hand, not before time if you ask me, and we can't go through to Dimerie today." He eyed the breakfast biscuit they were each munching and Hunston passed him one, then, seeing the guard's face, passed one out to him too.

"Mm, ta." The driver took a bite and carried on talking, munching between phrases, "This guard here, mm, he says we can wait in Castle Fortune. Mmm, mmm. He says it's safe, but it's up to you. Mmm, mmm. Funny place, Castle Fortune. Mmm, mmm. We could just stay here, mm, but we'd have to stay in the bus, he says, mmm, mmm."

The four looked at each other.

"My orders were to press on to Dimerie," said Merlin, mainly to Hunston. He hadn't spoken to Harry or Victor once he had learned they weren't princelings. As an official messenger and also in his status as journeyman in Buckmore, Harry had thought him stupid, as a princeling ought to recognise status within other castles, but he ignored the slight and treated him with due deference. Victor didn't care one way or the other.

Hunston was used to giving orders and was as easy to deal with as Prince Lupin. Indeed, Harry thought, he could well be the next Crown Prince if he had understood Wash's bloodlines correctly in the discussion on the way to the Prancing Pony.

"I think we should take up the offer of sanctuary in Castle Fortune," Hunston said. "If Vexstein and Buckmore are engaging Dimerie (or rather the pirates) in armed conflict, then we should move to a position of safety. We might be more useful to them there as well."

The others nodded at him.

"OK, driver," Hunston continued, "Let's go to Castle Fortune, if you please."

The driver put his hand to his cap and got back into his seat. The armed guard got up beside him and the bus moved on.

***

"Right then, Bailey," said the General. "What do you make of the sack that's been hung out of the fourth floor window since we arrived?"

Bailey had been to look at the sack, in his capacity as Buckmore Runner.

"It was thought to have been put out between 09.15 and 09.30 this morning, sir," Bailey reported. "It appears to be a carrot sack, just a common or garden variety, sir. In my opinion, sir, it could be the only thing resembling a white flag that the occupants have."

"Good reasoning, young man. What do you think Robert?" and the General turned to a youngish person with shaggy hair standing next to him. He bore a striking resemblance to Baden.

"I agree sir. It would seem advisable to send a small party forward to ascertain whether it is a surrender or not. Perhaps a group of the 25th, sir?" Robert added.

"Mmm, 25th, eh. Yes, they're good at this sort of thing. You take them forward, then Robert, and take young Bailey with you to manage any negotiations." Having given his orders, the General of the Western Marches Light Infantry waved them away. Bailey followed Robert out of the tent and along the lines of armed people to the group in green jackets, the 25th Rifle Company.

Within a few minutes, eight fighting fit soldiers had started off towards the castle, accompanied by Robert and Bailey, who carried a piece of cloth to pass as a white flag of truce if necessary.

**

The doors on either end of the fourth floor room were flung open and two soldiers burst in through each of them, guns sweeping the room and stopping to cover the inmates, who clung together in fear near to the window out of which they had hung a sack.

"Er, hello, it's all right, we surrender," said Fred, nervously and stepping to the front of the group. "And we're not armed," he added.

The soldiers kept their weapons pointed at them but stepped sideways into the room to be followed by one more each, a further one staying outside to guard the entrance from anyone else arriving. They said nothing.

"Really, we're quite harmless. We have a Princess in our safe-keeping and an injured steward," Fred tried again.

One of the soldiers looked at Baden as he lay by the fire, still resting after his ordeals. The others maintained their positions. "Sir!" one of them called through the door.

Robert and Bailey walked in cautiously.

"Bailey!" chorused Fred, George, and a little behind them as he couldn't see quite as well, "Bailey!" said Baden in a relieved tone.

"Who are these people, Bailey?" asked Robert.

"Major Robert, may I present Princelings Fred and George of Marsh, currently in the grace of Prince Lupin of Buckmore, and over there, looking a bit injured, is Baden, Steward to Prince Lupin. Fred, perhaps you would present the rest of your party?"

Fred introduced the rest, starting with Princess Kira, who received a deep bow from both Robert and Bailey, and named the others, hesitating a bit over Sundance, whom he left till last.

"Mmm, Sundance, eh?" said Robert, looking closer at him. "Pleased to meet you, but I will conveniently forget you as soon as you need me to."

"Thanks," said Sundance, with a slight grimace.

Fred looked at George as if to say "What was that all about?"

"Give me a short summary of what's happened," Robert instructed Fred.

"We, that is, George, Kira, Arthur, Theo, Sundance and I, were captured by pirates but escaped from Castle Marsh where we had washed up separately after the storm. Well, no, Kira was a hostage that I released and brought with us after I had met King Ludo and Uncle Vlad." He looked at Robert wondering if that was too much detail, but Robert just nodded at him to carry on. "We left La Boucherie in a hurry yesterday and took refuge here, where this morning we found Baden and the others trapped in a cellar. Baden and Dougall had received injuries fighting the pirates in the courtyard, and Princess Kira has attended to them. We didn't have a white flag, I'm afraid," he added, hoping he'd covered everything.

"Right," said Robert and turned to Baden. "Can you walk and do you need further attention?"

Baden said he could, and he probably didn't need further attention but maybe some healing balm would be helpful.

"I think those of you that are not going to be useful in our plans to defeat the pirates should stay here and organise the others, who will doubtless need to be organised once the fighting starts. We will also need a hospital wing."

Robert looked at Kira. "We have medicos, but it would be invaluable if you could organise that, your highness. I can send the medicos up and they will advise what is needed, but they aren't the best organisers."

"Send them to me," said Kira firmly, nodding.

"Sir," called one of the soldiers from the window. "The Dimerie bus is coming towards the castle gates."

"Thank you, Haggis," said Robert. He called over to one of the other soldiers by the door. "Neeps, go and escort the passengers up here, if you will, and advise the driver to see to his horses and then join the party in the store room at the gates."

The soldier disappeared out of the room and they heard him going down the stairs.

"What's going to happen next?" asked Baden.

"You and ... Dougall, was it? will stay here and recover your strength. Have any of the rest of you got combat experience?"

Most shook their heads but Lance said he could shoot a gun, had only done hunting though. Arthur looked worried, a fact that Robert didn't miss.

"Yes, thank you, my man, we are going up as fast as we can!" came a voice echoing up the stairs. Robert moved towards the door slightly to make sure the newcomers were moved right inside to join the rest.

"Who have we here?" he asked.

Neeps replied, "These 'ere are the trav'llers in the coach, this gent's a princelin' from 'umber, this one from Wash. These two're a bit quicker on the uptake," he said, bringing Harry and Victor into the room.

"Harry!" said Bailey.

"Victor!" said Fred and George at the same time as Bailey.

"OK, well they seem to be vouched for," said Robert. "Do any of you four have combat experience?"

"I do, Major," said Princeling Hunston, who obviously recognised Robert's sash markings. "These two," he said gesturing at Victor and Harry, "played a valiant part in the capture of a pirate ship off Wash the day before yesterday."

"OK, then," said Robert. "You three will come with me, and so will you, you, you, and you two." He pointed in turn at Theo, Sundance, Lance, Fred and George. "The rest of you will assist Princess Kira in organising the hospital facilities and also this rest room for non-combatants. I'll have supplies sent in to you, make sure you ration them. Assume you'll have "at least fifty more people here for at least a week."

"A week!" squeaked Arthur.

"You can leave things in my hands," said Princeling Merlin.

"Appreciated, but Baden is in command, with Princess Kira in charge of hospital and his number two. You've only just arrived and haven't done a recce yet. Happy to accept you as third in charge though," Robert added, which Merlin grudgingly accepted.

"Follow me!" he said to the others, and they filed out of the room.

***

Fred, George, Victor and Harry followed the soldiers in front of them as quietly as they could. They were all quite good at it; only Victor had not played at tracking or stalking when he was young, and although he bumped into things from time to time, he managed to do it quietly. They had been attached to the 25th temporarily, and although the regular soldiers looked at them as if they needed nursemaids, they had been kind enough and explained exactly what the soldiers were going to do, and what they expected the four of them to do as well. They didn't know where Theo, Lance and

Hunston had been sent, and Sundance had been sent off to the General's tent as soon as they had left the castle.

Fred was dying to know what Victor and Harry had been up to, but there was no time for that now. They were travelling quickly through the land towards a point west of Les Landes so they could come on the town, and the pirates, at the same time as the main assault down the open road. Their job was to make sure no pirates escaped along the cliff, or in any boat on the west side of the chateau. Fred would be going down the cliff with one of the soldiers, Haggis, he thought, to make sure any boats were disabled, and when they'd finished would patrol to capture any pirates trying to escape along the beach. The rest were going to patrol the cliff top, except for one brave soldier who was detailed to go along a goat track which hung precariously from the side of the cliff itself. The soldiers had talked of banging a stake in the cliff and roping him on to it before they had got close and fallen silent.

George was in the rear of the party, and feeling a little out of it. He didn't know whether he was up to the task of fighting anyone, and he wondered whether there might be time to set a trap for people to fall into. He thought a rope trap would be good if they had a little time, or an elephant trap if they had a lot of time. As they went through the vineyards he looked at the rows of grapes, now withering on the vines, and the buildings in the distance with four large cylindrical towers made of some sort of metal strapped to the outside of them. He wondered what sort of machines they used for making wine from grapes and hoped he'd have time for a look at them afterwards.

Harry concentrated on the road ahead, and kept an eye out for strangers and odd movements in the bushes or on the horizon. He had picked up a discarded sword and felt ready to go into battle like he had on the pirate ship. He hoped his opponent would be as unwilling to fight as the little guy had been on the Golden Guinea. He was paired up with Neeps and planned to stay as close to him as possible.

Victor ran along with the others, trying not to bump into things. He was enjoying the adventure but trying to work out how long he'd been away from the Inn and whether he was due to start his course work in a few days or whether he had a little longer. He was studying for a Masters in Business Administration and he didn't want his career in commerce to be cut short by a pirate. He decided he'd better concentrate a bit more when Fred stopped suddenly and he bumped into him.

Haggis got them all to gather round in the shade of an oak tree with plenty of greeny-bronze leaves still on it.

"OK, it'll be dark in less than an hour. We'll take up

our positions now – you can see the cliff edge over there," he pointed, "and this oak makes a good landmark so we can rendezvous back here afterwards. You can see the dust on the road over there," they looked and saw the dust rising, "so the army isn't far away. Baker, get down the cliff path now – him and me will go down to the beach," he finished, indicating Fred when he said "him". "Any questions?"

"Have I got time to set a few man-traps?" George asked.

"What do you need?" asked Haggis, interested.

"Some rope and ten minutes for a couple of simple noose traps, or two men, some spades and half an hour and some branches for an elephant trap," he replied.

"Neeps," said Haggis, "sort out a couple of simple noose traps with these guys, you haven't got time for an elephant trap. Do as many as you can. A simple head-line would be good too – say between those two trees – but make sure you all remember it's there. We'll be off."

So saying he and Fred went along to the cliff edge and peered over, then moved west along the top.

"There should be a winding path down near a headland scarred with white rock," he said.

"How do you know all this?" Fred asked.

"Information from guys who have been down and back a few times. That Sundance is one, infiltrated the pirates and got taken onto the ships. We recognised him. Good thing not too many people have seen him."

"Who sent the army to Castle Fortune?" Fred asked while Haggis was in a talking mood.

"Orders from above. Vexstein or Buckmore probably. Small army from Humber arrived as well, they've been put on the east side, I think. Should be easy enough for them there. This is the most likely way any pirates will try to escape – it's the most difficult terrain, so more likely they'll slip past unwary guards. Not us, though," he smiled grimly, as if relishing the evening's work. "Down here," he added as they came to a small break in the cliff with a very narrow, steep and rocky path, good for a goat. Fred was glad he'd enjoyed scrambling up and down Castle Marsh's rock face, he felt confident enough on these types of tracks.

He went down first, leading Haggis and not putting a foot wrong until near the bottom, when he found a sheer drop.

"We could back track to where it split round that thorn bush," he whispered, "or just jump."

Haggis pushed past and looked at the cliff. He undid his belt. "I'll lower you down," he said. "Then I'll jump and you can catch me."

Fred looked at him. "Can we do it the other way round?" he asked.

Haggis laughed. "OK!" he said, and giving Fred the buckle end of his belt, he went over the side, feeling with his feet for a bit, then said, "OK, take the weight" and Fred leant back, his feet sliding a bit as Haggis relied on the belt and stretched himself down as far as possible. Suddenly the belt went slack and Fred sat down hard on the ground. Haggis had dropped off the belt to the ground. Fred picked himself up and looked down for him. Haggis was rolling down a bit of sandy rubble at the base of the cliff, and then he got to his feet. He looked up.

"OK!" he called softly.

Fred looked down. He wished he'd gone first as Haggis had suggested, but then, the idea of Haggis launching himself to be caught by Fred had not been attractive. He looked at Haggis, counted to himself, one, two, three, and launched himself into the air, stretching out his arms and feet in the hope of slowing himself down a bit, and landed splat on top of Haggis, who rolled backwards with all the air knocked out of him.

They each sat up and rubbed various bits of themselves, then grinned at each other and got to their feet.

"Right, the boats!" said Haggis, and they ran along the beach, jumping over fallen boulders and rocky outcrops, until they could see a few boats drawn up onto the beach and tied onto stakes driven into a natural harbour among the rocks.

"Untie those and push them out while I see to the others," said Haggis, running on towards the ones on the beach. Fred climbed down into the cove and untied the boats, pushing them out into the sea. One of them hit a rock as it went and splintered in two. The others were caught by the waves and started moving out on the current. He ran back to Haggis. The light was fading fast now.

"We'll take up our station by that rock over there where the beach is narrowest," said Haggis, moving over to it. "Remember, try not to let anyone get past, and if in doubt send them over my way. Watch your footing on this rock. Take a good look at it so you have an idea of where to stand and fight."

Fred nodded, breathless from the action so far, and nervous of what was to come. He could hear noises from the town now, and the sound of marching on the road was strangely cut off when he took two paces back round the rock, then reappeared when he went back to it. Suddenly the marching noise went but a rushing noise followed it, a sound as if all the army had surged forward to attack. They could hear shouts and screams as well.

"With any luck, the 2nd came round this side in a flanking movement so we'll only get what they missed," said Haggis. Fred nodded, not sure what it meant, but hoping it was a good thing.

"Draw your sword," said Haggis, drawing his and laying it beside him, and then taking aim with his gun. He shot once, reloaded and shot again, and again, then slung his gun upside down over his back and picked up his sword.

"That'll scare a couple up the cliff: here we go!" and he stepped forward as two pirates ran towards them. Fred moved to the seaward side and brandished his sword and they ran up towards the cliff, unwilling to meet them head on. A few more had seen their colleagues fall as a result of Haggis's shots and had turned up towards the cliff. Others yelled "the boats, the boats" and, realising the boats had gone, turned and ran back into the ones still approaching.

"Looks like they've run out of ammo," commented Haggis, and he leant down and loaded his gun once more, getting off a couple more shots. Even though they weren't very close together, the shots deterred the pirates, and they were clambering up the hillside. Two fell down and tumbled to the bottom of the cliff. "Get them!" hissed Haggis, and Fred ran over to them, sword raised.

"No, we surrender, we surrender," pleaded the pirates, dropping their swords and kneeling at Fred's feet. He pointed his sword at them, picked up their swords and threw them into the sea, then grabbed one's handkerchief off his head and tied his wrists while keeping the other one down by standing on his back. Then, ripping off his sleeve which was half torn already, Fred secured the second one.

He looked back, wondering what to do about their feet, and saw Haggis fighting three at once, and winning easily. Their bodies he kicked into the sea. He looked along the beach once more, and could see no-one running. All the noise was on the cliff top or on the other side of the town. He looked back at his captives.

"Up," he said, gesturing with his sword. They got to their feet and he drove them towards Haggis.

"These two surrendered. What shall I do with them?" he asked.

Haggis pulled some cord out from around his waist.

"Walk them to the edge of town, then sit them down and tie their feet. Then join me back on the cliff. They'll be found by dawn. Make sure they can't undo each other," and he gave Fred the cord and started back up the cliff himself.

Fred pushed the two captives forward and they reached the edge of the town with no mishap other than a few stumbles on the part of the pirates. As he got there he found a convenient signpost and got the two to stand either side of it, with their backs to each other, tying one man's left leg to the other's right, so they were attached to the post, and couldn't reach their feet to untie each other. Then for good measure, and because there was more rope than he had used, he looped the end up around their waists and pulled it tight so they couldn't bend down easily either. Satisfied, he wished them luck, told them if they had really surrendered they'd be ok, and then sped off back up the cliff top to see what more he could do there.

It was now fully dark, and he moved cautiously, remembering they'd been planning various traps. He could hear some scuffling over towards the heather covered area, but he was aiming mainly for the outline of the oak tree in the darkness. He was getting quite close when someone jumped on him and started hitting him with the side of his sword. "Ow!" he said.

"Take that!" the assailant replied.

"Victor?" he asked, recognising the voice.

"Who's that?" said Victor, stopping.

"It's Fred! Ouch, thanks. How are you?"

"Fine, it's really exciting. Thought you were a pirate," said Victor.

"Yeah, I realised," said Fred grinning, for he wasn't at all hurt, and if that had been Victor's assault on all the pirates he'd met, neither were they! "Where is everyone?"

"Not sure. Got a bit lost. Where's the tree. Do you know?" he finished.

Fred looked, then crouched down to see if he could get any outline of the oak tree with the deep blue of the sky behind it. The moon was just rising in the east, but it was not full enough to make a difference with the thin cloud around.

"I think it's this way," he said at last.

They made their way through the bushes and short grass at the top of the cliff and down into a grass-lined dell with a tree on its western side. It wasn't the right one.

"Can you hear any of the others?" Fred asked, and they listened carefully.

"No," replied Victor. "Tree over there though." And he pointed to another tree showing just above a pile of rocks.

"Take care in case there's a trap," said Fred softly, and they moved cautiously in that direction.

"Halt, who goes there?" hissed a voice and Fred felt a prod in his middle, possibly made by a sword or a gun.

"Fred of Marsh," he said.

"Victor," said Victor.

"Pass friend," said the voice, and one of the soldiers came round a bush and looked at them more closely. "I'll take you to the others. Follow me closely."

He led them to the tree and then returned to his sentry post. Four soldiers were sitting around, cleaning their weapons.

"Good," said Neeps. "That's two of you safe an' sound."

"Where are George and Harry?" asked Fred.

"'aggis an' Chad are searchin'," replied Neeps.

"Did you capture many pirates?" Fred thought all the soldiers were accounted for if two were on sentry duty, so wondered where the prisoners were.

"I don' think any got away, put it tha' way," said Neeps. "Ask no questions, tell no lies."

Fred sat down and rubbed his shoulder, which hurt a bit now he had stopped doing things. He wished he had a drink, and some food. One of the soldiers passed him a flask as he wished it and he took a swig, coughed violently, wondered who had set fire to his mouth and throat, then took another swig to make it feel better. That worked, he thought. Then he wondered where George had got to. The idea of making traps had been brilliant, and much better suited to his talents than fighting. Maybe he had taken captives down to the town too, he thought.

After a few more minutes there was a rustle in the undergrowth. Three of the soldiers stood up and moved forward. He heard some low murmuring, then two came back carrying something, and another two emerged carrying something else. Haggis brought up the rear. They laid their burdens down carefully in the centre of the grass and stepped back.

Fred stood up and gasped. Lying in the pale moonlight, eyes closed, limp and lifeless, were Harry and George.

Chapter 11: Aftermath

In which Fred returns to Castle Fortune and Lupin meets his future bride

Baden helped Kira with another still body that had been loaded onto the wagons to be brought back to the hospital. Most were suffering from concussion but some had more serious injuries, especially sword wounds. Kira was looking through them, working out who should jump the queue to get professional attention, who would be enough with her care, and who could wait altogether. Baden was very handy with bandages by now.

He checked another one in; they were getting near to the end of the wagons now, and he hoped not too many would come in as they had worked all through the night. Every now and then he had checked someone, tested their pulse, listened for a heartbeat and shaken his head and they'd been taken back onto a wagon to go to a long line of people covered with blankets. Relatives might want to claim the bodies and in any case, they all had to be named and their castles informed. He sighed. It was a sad business. He looked over at Kira working tirelessly, but saw the lines of grief etched on her face amongst the grey of weariness.

"Only two more wagon loads, Kira. You can take a break then."

"But there are those who need nursing, Baden. I can't stop until they have been settled," she replied, with a grateful smile.

She gestured for one to be moved up closer to the head of the queue and they started unloading the second to last wagon.

"This has been up on the cliff top, sir," the wagon driver said to Baden. "There be two soldiers, the rest be pirates."

"We'll look at them all, driver," said Baden, "We must aid the pirates as well, you know."

"Aye, sir," responded the driver, "but these two here be the soldiers."

Baden stood stock still as he looked first at George and then at Harry. He stepped forward and checked

George over. He was breathing shallowly and his pulse was faint but rapid. "Kira!" he called.

She looked at George and bent forward to look at his head. There was a large lump on the side of it just behind his ear, but she could see no sign of bleeding. "Serious head injury, severe trauma, unconscious, go right to the front of the queue!" she ordered the helpers, who lifted George's stretcher off the wagon and took him up to the medicos.

She turned to Baden, who was bent over Harry, checking for a pulse, a heartbeat, a breath. He looked up at her sadly. "You check," he said tonelessly.

Kira checked him over, and couldn't find a pulse either. His hands were cold. She tried breathing into his mouth to see if her breath would promote breathing in him. She tried for a minute or two, but nothing happened. "I'm sorry, Baden," she said, looking up at him. "If he was alive when he was put on the wagon, he's gone now. Did you know him?"

Baden nodded. "Journeyman of Buckmore," he managed to get out through a constricted voice. "We sent him to solve the riddle of the lack of Dimerie wines."

He turned away, and then remembered there were others to attend to. He asked the helpers to put Harry in a side room, claimed already, and they did so, while he went back to unloading the pirates and then the injured on the last wagon.

Although the hospital base was still Castle Fortune, and many of the ordinary soldiers had returned to their camp there, the General and his staff had moved on to an encampment just outside Les Landes, in a pleasant park adjacent to the winery. They had been joined by Prince Lupin and Lord Smallweed, come down from Buckmore and Vexstein drawn by the latest messages, not least the intelligence from Bailey and from King Lynn, and the need to have a proper regal presence for the trial of King Ludo.

The personnel at Chateau Dimerie had been liberated in the early hours of the morning, and Princess Nerys had invited all to stay at the chateau as soon as the place could be made habitable again, the pirates having made a truly disgusting mess of everything once they had thrown her in the dungeon with Baden and the others. Meanwhile, the guest quarters at the winery had been pressed into action for Lord Smallweed and his entourage, while Prince Lupin said he was young and fit enough to camp with the officers.

Now they were gathering round a large tented area, awaiting the arrival of King Helier, Princess Nerys, and any of her brothers who could be located amongst the many who had taken up arms against the pirates, so that the trial could begin.

The general tapped his fingers irritably.

"Why don't they come?" he asked to no-one in particular.

"It may be the tide, sir," responded one of his aides-de-camp.

"They could use boats!"

"I think the boats were all used by the pirates, sir, and therefore destroyed by our troops to ensure they didn't escape in them." Robert had joined them, and he knew more about this than most, having ordered the action in which this happened.

"Bah!" responded the general.

Lupin and Smallweed came over to join him and take places on the table at the head of the room.

"It was an excellent strategy you devised, General," said Lupin soothingly. "It is inevitable that some inconveniences arise out of a well-devised action."

Smallweed just looked at them, then asked if there was anything to drink after their long and tiring journey. Lupin allowed himself a hint of a smile at his peevishness, then a slightly broader smile as a crate of Vex beer arrived, the bottles being duly opened and handed round by Robert.

"Have you seen anything of your brother, Robert?" Lupin asked.

"Yes indeed, sire," Robert responded. "He is in Castle Fortune, recovering from a head injury received during the flight from Chateau Dimerie where he was imprisoned for a time. I understand he is helping with the sick and wounded there."

"Hm," said Lupin. "I need to speak with him. You haven't seen either of the young princelings from Marsh, have you?"

"Yes, sire, one of them is in the ante-room at present, waiting to be called for the trial."

"Waiting to be called? Only in evidence I hope!"

"Yes, sire, but also to sit and hear the entire trial as of course it has a major bearing on his future," Robert elaborated.

"Can I see him now, I would like to hear his news. As long as it doesn't prejudice the trial, of course," Lupin added.

"It would probably be best if you could wait, sire," was Robert's cautious reply, and Lupin sat back and drank his Vex.

*** *

The trial was over. It had taken most of the day even though the Dimerie party had arrived as soon as the tide had cleared the causeway, late in the morning. Now a long table had been set out in the garden outside the tent, serving fresh fruit, wine and some special dishes devised by the local hostelries they thought the nobles would enjoy.

King Ludo had been deposed and banished, with Uncle Vlad continuing as Regent in his place until the line of succession could be formally established. Vladimir had made a deposition by express messenger apologising to all present but explaining that, as Regent, he had to act as directed by his king, although he had exercised his best judgement to minimise the extent of his nephew's depredations.

A series of misdemeanours had been pressed upon a number of pirates who elected to go with King Ludo into exile, and the rest of those still on the mainland were considered to be either in temporary custody at Castle Fortune, or free to go about their business and mend their ways, provided they could find castles willing to repatriate them. As a result, a motley crowd of ex-pirates were currently standing in lines in front of tables where officials of the major castles were hearing cases already.

Baden had been brought down from his work at Castle Fortune to hear cases at the Castle Buckmore table, and was presently hearing a plea from a young man called Pippin. He expressed interest in navigation and had heard tell of a philosopher carrying out mapping work at Buckmore to whom he would willingly offer his services. Baden thought this far-fetched but gave the young man a temporary pass simply because he seemed energetic and intelligent.

He had also brought the good news to Fred that George was still alive, at least when he had left Castle Fortune, although he had not yet regained his senses. Fred had left to go straight to his side, despite Baden's advice that Lupin wanted an urgent talk with him in private.

"I'll be at Castle Fortune," he said.

Lupin was socialising with the other kings, and taking the opportunity to speak to Princess Nerys, who was still willing to visit, but wondered whether Prince Lupin would be willing for her to delay her trip until such time as her father could spare her. There was a great deal for her and her brothers to do in order to re-establish order at the chateau, she said. Lupin had graciously agreed, although he admired her courage and fortitude during this ordeal and had said so. "Oh it was nothing," she had said, "you should hear what my sister went though and is still doing," and she had elaborated on Kira's deeds and selflessness even now in dealing with the wounded.

∗

Fred went back to Castle Fortune with the 25th, who were happy to have him with them, and gave him much comradeship to ease his burden. Victor came too, although he was eager to continue on home to the Inn and hoped he would be able to find a bus going back that way. Baker and Neeps were detailed to escort Victor back up as far as the Bridge Inn to wait for a bus, while Haggis took Fred up to the Castle.

"Good luck mate," he said as they parted. "We're at your service, and your brother's, any time you need us." Fred nodded and went inside.

The Castle looked totally different from when he had left it. It was now a hive of activity, people everywhere, going in and out, a small market stall in the yard, fresh juices being dispensed to weary travellers and recovering combatants. He picked up a strawberry juice, then two celery juices, and made his way through the courtyard to go up to the room he had left such a long time ago, although it was only the previous day. He had a vague idea that was where he would find George, and he hoped to find Kira too, to find out how she was doing.

He stepped into the room and found he was in a hospital ward, with his little fire still glowing in the fireplace, looking particularly welcoming as he walked towards it. A nurse sat at its side gazing into the flames.

"Excuse me," he said, "I'm looking for my brother George and also for Princess Kira."

The nurse looked up. "Well, you've found us both, Fred," said Kira. "George is right here." And she indicated the bed next to the fire where someone lay with his head covered in bandages.

Fred stepped over to him. "George," he whispered, peering into the slit in the bandages allowing him to see. "I brought you a celery juice."

"Here, let me," said Kira, and she wound back some of the lower bandages and produced a straw, angling the cup and the straw so George could drink.

"He's not allowed to speak yet, even if he can. The medicos want him fully bandaged today but say they will check him in the morning and they expect the swelling to have gone down sufficiently for him just to need a direct pressure bandage."

"Will he be all right?" whispered Fred with the worried look that had haunted him since the night before still etched on his face.

"Probably, but it may take time for him to recover all his abilities, and some may be impaired. We don't know yet. It's very early yet, Fred." And Kira took his arm and led him back to a seat by the fire, handing him his strawberry juice. "Who is this celery juice for?"

"Um, you if you'd like it," he said, thinking of George. She smiled at him and sipped it gratefully.

"Where are you staying tonight?" Kira asked.

"Right here, I think," said Fred, not looking away from the fire.

"The bed next to George is free, use that."

And when Prince Lupin arrived later in the evening to see him, he found Fred and George asleep in adjacent beds, and Princess Kira curled up asleep in a blanket by the fire.

Chapter 12: The Line of Succession

In which Fred has a good talk to Lupin, and George has a headache

The sound of rain beating on the windows echoed through the room and what passed for daylight stole along the corridors. Princess Kira rose and stretched. A quick glance around showed her lots of sleeping patients and two sleeping beauties: Fred asleep next to George, looking drawn still, but a better colour than the day before, and Lupin curled up in a blanket next to the fire across from her corner. She moved quietly to George's bedside.

"Are you awake, George?" she asked quietly, putting her head close to his so he could hear through the bandages. He raised a hand.

"Are you hungry?" The hand was raised twice.

"Very, eh? I'll have to see the medicos first and let them sort you out, but I'll bring you something nice. There's celery juice here still – would you like it?" she added, and George raised his hand again for 'yes, please'. Kira wound back his lower bandage again and helped him to sip through the straw. Small noises started to come up to the windows from the courtyard below, and Kira reckoned the castle was starting to wake up. She wondered whether anyone had seen the ghost/Rumour during the night. She hadn't heard of any encounters with him since the start of the battle and she wondered whether all the activity had frightened him away.

By the fire Lupin moved and stretched, and unwound himself from the blanket. Kira looked over at him as she continued to hold the juice cup for George. He looked at her.

"I really need a strong hot drink," he said.

A knock came on the door, and Neeps put his head round.

"Beg pardon, Princess," he said to Kira. "we wuz just wonderin' 'ow our George is farin'. And we brought 'ot tea in case you needed some."

"George is coming along well, thank you," replied Kira. "He's just taking some celery juice, look. With any luck he'll only have to have a small bandage on for the rest of the day."

"Shall I look after the tea for you?" said Lupin, getting up hopefully.

"We've only got this one big can, but it'll be okey-dokey if you don' mind passin' it round," said Neeps, handing it over. "Blimey! Ain't you Prince-King Lupin our big boss?"

"Yes I'm afraid I am," said Lupin with a sigh, "and you might well be promoted for bringing me tea in my hour of need."

"I don't wan' no promotion, thank you kindly sir. But me and my mates would like a perm'nent station, perhaps at Castle Buckmore, if you could arrange it sir, bein' so bold to ask, sir," Neeps added, trying to temper impertinence with politeness.

Lupin smiled. "I'll see what I can do. How did Fred do in the battle?" he asked, waving to Fred asleep in the next bed still.

"Blimey, he's not hurt is he? We thought he was ok?" said Neeps, concern flashing into his eyes.

"He's fine," Kira reassured him with a smile. "He was just exhausted, not used to all this, plus worrying about his brother of course."

"And King Ludo, I'll bet, what with comin' from Marsh an' all. I wonder who'll be king there now?"

"We all wonder that," said Lupin, switching his gaze from George to Fred, and then to Kira, for some unfathomable reason.

"Right, I'll be off then," said Neeps, "If you'll be so kind to get the can back to the quar'master, I'd be right glad, your majesty, sir."

"I'll do that very thing," said Lupin with a smile, "Thanks for thinking of us, er, Neeps isn't it? Of the 25th?"

"Yes, sir," replied Neeps, straightening up with pride at being recognised by so esteemed a personage. "I'll go then." He backed out of the door and they could hear him talking to his mates as they went down the stairs.

"I think he'll talk about his chat with you by the fireside for weeks," smiled Kira. "Will you get them a permanent station somewhere?"

"I may, but I need to talk to Fred first. I have an idea that would work well, but there are so many problems to sort out, Kira."

"I'm sure they are, but what is your main one?"

"The line of succession at Castle Marsh."

George coughed and spluttered a bit as if some celery juice had gone down the wrong way, and Kira turned back to tend to him. While she was doing so, Lupin rose and went out of the door, to do some thinking from one of the Castle's many towers.

***

Fred woke, stared at the ceiling, and remembered where he was and what had been going on. He sat bolt upright and saw George, lying in the bed next to him, but not wrapped up like he had been the night before, just with a simple bandage round his head holding a pressure pad in place behind his ear.

"Are you ok?" he asked him.

George smiled and raised a hand. Kira saw the movements from the other side of the room and came to join them.

"He's doing fine, Fred," she said, "but he can't talk at present. The medicos say it's a temporary thing, but as far as they can tell all his other faculties are perfectly normal."

George grinned and grunted.

"Even for you, mate," Fred said, looking at him and grinning too, and George raised a hand in agreement.

"Why can't he talk?" he asked Kira.

"It's something to do with pressure from the lump brought up by the bash on the head. It's affecting the part of his brain that manages speech," she explained. "He probably phrases words perfectly in his head, but the instructions to his mouth just aren't working. It may be temporary, or he may need to learn how to speak again over a longer period of time."

Fred looked at him again, concern etched in his face, then it cleared and he grinned again. "Going to be quiet around here for a while, then!"

Prince Lupin came into the room.

"Ah, good, you're awake. Would you care to take a walk with me and we'll find you some breakfast on the way?" he asked, and Fred got out of bed to go with him.

They went down the back stairs to the kitchens, where they found fresh bread and a speciality of the area, lovely buttery rolls. They also smelled some distinctive biscuits being made so they would be ready for the afternoon meal, called Cookies.

"Where have all these people come from?" asked Fred, munching a roll.

"The news that the castle is not actually haunted has helped, plus the elimination of the pirates and a number of the other rogues in the area. The presence of Princess Kira has put heart into people, which is a bit of a complication, but there is also some hope that we can go through the lines of succession to find a valid heir to the castle and install him, at least on a temporary basis."

Fred felt like asking why Princess Kira couldn't rule the castle, since she would be jolly good at it, and the people obviously supported her, but suddenly thought he didn't want to suggest that, not at the moment, anyway.

They wound their way up one of the towers for a

view of the surrounding area. Fred approved of the view, and said so.

"I know you like to have a view when you're Thinking," Lupin remarked.

"What do you want me to think about?" asked Fred, looking at him suspiciously.

"King Ludo and Castle Marsh," replied Lupin.

"He's gone, hasn't he? Why think of him?"

"Who is to replace him at Castle Marsh, Fred?"

"I thought Uncle Vlad had been appointed Regent till the heir was found," Fred said.

"Exactly," said Lupin with a grim smile, "and who is the rightful heir? I'd like to know your thoughts on the family tree before the legal people get involved. They'll be here later, along with my experts and Vladimir himself."

"Oh," said Fred, pouting a bit. "I hope we get on better than we did the other day."

"There are some big questions to ask. Did Ludo have any sons that can be classed as of royal blood? What is Vlad's line of descent from the nearest relatives? Which princelings of King Cole's line are still alive and can provide a claim? If none, then whose line is the next in priority? And where do you and George fit in the line of Succession?"

Fred pouted some more and gazed out of the window. "I don't like the last question," he said, "and I have a feeling that you're leading me down a line of questions I'm not going to like the answers to."

"Nevertheless, they do need to be answered, Fred," said Lupin, "which is why my experts will be here to help you. They are pretty good at helping unwilling heirs wriggle through the rules a bit."

Fred looked at him. "You're really the king of Buckmore, aren't you?" he said.

"Um, yes," said Lupin with a sigh. "I didn't think you'd realised. Baden said you hadn't when you were leaving Buckmore to come on this journey."

"No, I hadn't till just now, or maybe when the trial was on yesterday all the clues were presented to me at the same time and I've worked them out in my sleep. That's why you have to find a suitable bride."

"I didn't want to be king. I enjoy being a prince, going round the land, meeting people, not being stuck in the castle with a load of toadying hangers-on. But I've found it doesn't have to be like that, and I've grown to enjoy some of the responsibilities and powers. I think Ludo has the same problem, although his biggest problem is enjoying sailing and being a mischief-maker. If he got himself organised on land we would have discord throughout the country, so it's just as well he took to being a pirate. He couldn't rule in harmony with the rest of us.

Baden says the best kings are the reluctant ones, but maybe Ludo has changed his view. He's one of my experts, by the way."

"Why?"

"He and his brother had the most recent experiences of a challenge to the line of succession at Powell. They are very hot on the legalities but also the possibilities. In the end, both of them managed to avoid being swamped by the politics of the situation, Baden by being out of Powell long enough to relinquish his claim, and Robert by joining the army in a senior position, which according to the statute on the founding of the army, automatically and irrevocably disqualifies officers from holding court at their castle. Prevents armed coups," Lupin finished abruptly.

Fred gazed out of the window once more. He mentally compared the views from here with those at Marsh and at Buckmore. They were all pretty good, he thought. Where were he and George in terms of the line of succession?

"Is this place really haunted?" asked Lupin, breaking his train of thought.

"I think it is, but by a mad, or at least extremely antisocial, old retainer of the Fortune family, called Rumour," explained Fred. "We think we saw him on the top floor the other evening, and certainly someone of the same description shut Baden and the others in the dungeon here."

"We need to find him," said Lupin.

Without them doing anything, the door to the stairway swung open. They looked at each other and started towards it.

"Lupin," Fred asked cautiously, "do you ever say 'I need something' and it suddenly appears?"

Lupin looked at him. "Er, well, I've never told anyone else, but yes, sort of. Like this morning when I woke I said I needed a strong hot drink, and one of the soldiers arrived with a can of tea for us to share. Does it happen to you?"

"Yes, like that fire in the room, which has been burning since I said I needed it the first day we arrived, and hasn't had any logs added," Fred said, "and the tunnel from Castle Marsh to the time tunnel," he added.

"Impressive!" said Lupin, "I've never had really important things like that. Um, don't tell anyone else," he added.

"Well, we've always felt it would prove I'm peculiar!" Fred laughed.

"George knows?" Fred nodded. "Does he do it?" Lupin asked.

"No, not that we've ever tried, I don't think," Fred replied. "He seemed to think it was my speciality."

"Interesting. Fred, I think there is a good chance you may be a legitimate heir of Castle Marsh. Let's see whether this castle is going to lead us to Rumour, then we can talk some more about it," and they started down the stair. They passed the level they came in at and continued down till another door swung open for them. They reckoned they were below ground, but not as far as the vaults, maybe on the servants' level. They went along a couple of corridors and through other doors that swung open as they approached. Finally they reached a door which opened onto a very narrow spiral staircase going up a very narrow tower a very long way.

It opened into a small room right under the eves of the turret. On the furthest side from the door was a large bundle of greyish white wool. They went over and looked at it. It was moving very slightly, as if it was breathing.

"Rumour," called Fred softly. "Wake up Rumour, we need you."

The eye nearest them opened and blinked. Then it closed again and the body sort of shuffled about on its blankets.

"Rumour," said Lupin. "Your master needs you."

"Master gone," said the person in a croaky voice. "New people come. No use for Rumour now." And he shuffled about again to ignore them.

"We need Princess Kira here," Lupin said, "she's of the royal blood of Fortune."

They stood looking at Rumour, who in truth did not look very well, and then they heard footsteps on the stairs.

"Hello?" came Kira's voice.

Fred and Lupin looked at each other then Fred went to the door to escort her in.

"Why did you come here?" asked Lupin gently.

"There are people waiting on you, Prince Lupin, and I had a feeling I might be able to find you. I don't know why, I've never been up here before." She looked at the pile of wool. "Is that Rumour?" she asked.

"Yes, we couldn't get him to pay any attention to us," Lupin said. "Can you persuade him to come down?"

She went over to him and put her hand on his shoulder. "Rumour, it's Princess Kira. I'm sorry we left you alone for so long. Would you like to come down and look after me?"

Rumour looked at her, then got slowly to his feet and shook himself. He was old and unsteady on his feet. "What does mistress require of me?" he asked her in a wobbly voice.

"Come with me to the hospital wing and let me look after you till you're well," she said, half a request and half an order. She turned and led the way, Rumour following her like a well trained person would. Fred and Lupin followed, shutting doors behind them.

***

Vladimir sat in a chair in the main hall, which was cleared of debris and tidied up so a Council of Kings could take place. Glasses of Chateau Dimerie wine stood on the table, along with piles of papers in front of the lawyers and a long scroll which stretched from Lord Smallweed at one side, past Fred, George (still bandaged and with a blanket round him), Lupin, Robert and Baden, Hunston who had proved himself most valiant in the battle, and who was recognised as Crown Prince by all the other nobles, to King Helier of Dimerie at the other.

"So you see, my lords," said Vladimir. "Ludo was a direct descendent and resident heir, and legitimately the king of Marsh when Cole died."

Fred had tackled Lupin about this issue when they had got back downstairs. Why had no-one at Buckmore informed Fred and George their king had died in the late summer? He had looked horribly embarrassed and shifted from foot to foot. He explained, very badly, that they meant to, but Fred and George seemed to be having so much fun, and George was so involved with his experiments, so they put it off for a week, and then something else came up and they forgot, and then Baden reminded them that nothing had been said, and then it seemed so horribly late to do so. "And you hadn't seemed too worried about the situation at Marsh, really," Lupin finished lamely. Fred had sighed in exasperation, and wondered whether it really made any difference and what he would have done had he known. The more he thought, the more he thought it made no difference, and eventually he told Lupin he forgave him. What George thought no-one knew. All he had indicated was that his head hurt, and he was happy to keep as still as possible. He was trying to take an interest in the genealogy scroll, but didn't want to move his head to look down, so tended to just shut his eyes and listen to what was being said around him. Now they were involved in the discussion of who should be the legitimate king at Marsh.

There was general murmuring at Vlad's statement, and the legal eagles looked up and said, yes, that looked right to them, and Smallweed added his agreement, and so on round the table. Fred and George's opinions were not sought, nor were those of Baden or Robert.

"But Ludo left no heir, that is right isn't it, Vladimir," asked Smallweed, "so does succession not go to the offspring of his brothers?"

The legal eagles and Vlad nodded.

"So we have Cornelius..." Smallweed read off.

"Died a year ago," Vlad said, "leaving the four daughters."

"Gamesman..."

"Left four years ago, not seen since."

"... Locksley..."

"Last heard of causing trouble in the northern woods, but not been to Castle Marsh for years," said Vlad.

"... then Ludo. And only Princess Molly had any male offspring from the whole lot of them. Unusual," he sniffed.

"So as Cole only had the one son from whom this lot came," recapped King Helier, shifting so he could get a better view of the scroll, "we have to look at his own brothers."

"It may be that we have to look at Ludo's heir through the female lines," said one of the legal advisers somewhat quietly, but Lord Smallweed and King Helier showed no reaction if they heard him. Lupin and Baden's eyes met and they grinned at each other.

"So Cole was Rudolph's only son out of ... Alpheria, is that?" asked Helier.

"Yes," confirmed Vlad, adding, "he then married Anastasia and had Boris and myself ..."

"... then Arthur," Smallweed interrupted, his finger moving along the scroll's bloodline.

"Died ten years ago in a shooting accident," said Vlad. "Sons by Princess Gabby emigrated to the west twelve years ago, sons by Princess Molly, who was Ludo's sister, Fred and George here present."

"But you left over six months ago, didn't you?" asked Lord Smallweed of Fred.

"Yes your lordship, although I visited last week and met King Ludo and Uncle Vlad," Fred explained, deciding he ought to make this clear, "and George was received into the castle, although did not see Ludo or Uncle Vlad, but they knew he was there."

The legal people muttered and started flicking through their papers, murmuring to each other.

"So unless Fred or George succeed it goes to Cole's first brother: Boris," stated the lawyer, looking to Lord Smallweed, who frowned.

"All of Boris's sons left the castle over three years ago," said Vlad. "Boris died four years ago and I have no idea whether any of his sons are alive or not."

The lawyers sighed, whilst Smallweed merely nodded.

"And the next brother was you, Vladimir." Smallweed finished the line on the scroll.

"Yes, that is correct," said Vlad simply.

"And you have no issue, is that right?"

"Yes, I have never married and have no intention of doing so."

"So if Fred and George have not forfeited their claim, you come into the reckoning. Yes?" asked Smallweed, and he turned to the lawyers.

"We, er, think that the forfeit is null, and that Fred is the legitimate heir, since the female line precedes the avuncular line," said the lawyers.

Fred's heart sank and George put his hand on his arm and squeezed it sympathetically.

"One moment, if you please," said Baden, flicking through papers of his own and with Robert whispering in his ear.

"Do these people speak on your behalf, Lupin?" asked one of the lawyers sternly, as if he knew Robert and Baden from the past and was hoping to get their input disregarded.

"Yes, they do." Lupin said firmly, and the lawyer who asked sank back dejectedly.

"How long had Ludo been king?" Baden asked.

"Just over two months," replied Vladimir.

"Does that not mean the principle of tenancy applies, and that Ludo's reign as king should not be confirmed?" stated Baden.

The lawyers all murmured again and delved into their papers in an agitated manner.

"Explain the principle of tenancy, if you please, Baden," sighed Lord Smallweed.

Baden double checked something with Robert, who pointed to a paragraph in a document.

Baden stood up and read; "If a king shall not hold the reign for a period of three successive months, the principle of tenancy deems that he shall not establish his line, and that his successor shall not follow the normal rules. The line of succession shall revert to the previously established king."

"What does that mean, please?" asked Smallweed somewhat plaintively.

"The principle was established at a time when usurpation was rife and intrigue meant that some kings were installed and bumped off in order to get specific people onto the throne," Baden explained. "If a king did not reign for three successive months he is deemed not to have succeeded, and the line of succession returns to the next in line from the last legitimate king."

"So who does that make it?" asked Helier.

"I think that makes Vladimir here king of Castle Marsh, although if he dies without a son of his own, then Fred is the next in line." Baden finished, whispering to Fred, "stay of execution, old chap, best I could offer." Fred gave him a wry smile. George patted Fred's arm.

The lawyers finished muttering and their leader stood up.

"This appears to be correct," he said. "Tenancy applies, and the fraternal line takes precedence over the female line," and he sat down again.

"So that means, if we are all agreed that the process is correct, that Vladimir becomes King Vladimir of Castle Marsh, and unless he has legitimate issue before he dies, that his heir presumptive is Fred." He looked at the lawyers, who nodded.

"All those in agreement, say 'Aye'," said Smallweed.

"Aye!" all the kings and the crown prince said.

"All those against, say 'Nay'," said Smallweed.

There was silence.

"Well, King Vladimir, congratulations!" and he reached for his glass of wine. "Long life and good health to King Vladimir!" he said and the others raised their glasses and echoed the toast.

They got up and pushed their chairs away from the table. Fred stayed seated with George beside him. Baden leaned over again.

"That does mean you'll need to keep visiting on a regular basis, at least once a year," he said, "in order to maintain your claim."

Fred nodded. "I think that'll be ok. We've always got on well with Uncle Vlad. I'd better go and say something to him."

He got up and went over to Vlad, who looked a little stunned by this turn of events.

"Well done, Uncle," Fred said when the crowd had dispersed a bit.

"Ah you unhappy about the outcome, young Fred?" he asked.

"Not at all, although with all this going on these past few weeks, and realising how desolate a castle can be when the line fails," he said waving at Castle Fortune around him, "I would rather give up my enjoyment than let that happen to Marsh."

Vlad looked at him. "I have always thought you and George were extremely clever young people with the capacity to become wise," he said. "I would be happy to name you crown prince if you like. I have no desire to take a wife at my age."

"Does it make a difference?" Fred asked.

"It does away with the absolute need to be present in the castle once a year, but I hope you would like to come anyway. I think you and George have plenty of good ideas for modernisation, if what I hear from Lupin is anything to go by. Think about it. We can discuss it when you next visit."

"I will," said Fred.

Chapter 13: Epilogue

In which Fred and George look forward to a happy new year

Fred gazed out of the window at the mountains behind Buckmore, looking at the snow-covered land and listening to the ice cracking off the dry grass in the ditches beyond the castle. His wind map lay completed behind him, as they had recovered far more data from their wind machines than they had ever expected, and George had helped him with the calculations while he waited for the delivery of four tall cylindrical towers from Dimerie for his strawberry juice experiment.

The Princesses Nerys and Kira were due to arrive tomorrow for their visit to Prince Lupin, which had been extended to two weeks (and therefore included both the Solstice and the Green Willow celebrations), a courtesy neither of the other princesses that had visited since Ruby's departure had been accorded. Baden was keen for Lupin to marry one of the Dimerie princesses, and the general view was that Lupin was keen to as well. Fred was quite keen for him to marry one of them, but not the other. He needed to talk to George about the subject. They had visited Castle Marsh for a week and he had agreed to become Vlad's crown prince. Now, knowing there was one lady he would want as his queen above all the others he had met, he wanted at least to come to an understanding with her if he could. He wondered what George would think.

George came into the room and waved his arms around a lot.

"Have you done it?" Fred asked him, grinning.

George nodded, and jumped up and down a bit.

"Aren't you a bit early?" Fred asked, referring to the fact that he still had a year to go until the secret of energy from strawberry juice would be revealed to the world.

George shook his head, no, and then used one hand to act as if he was turning a large wheel.

"Lots more stuff to do yet, then?"

George nodded, but smiled and sat beside him contentedly. He made some interesting noises as if he was trying to explain something, and Fred watched his lips carefully. He couldn't quite make out what George was saying yet, but he was definitely improving. He wondered whether Kira would help him with his speech while she was here, although Lady Nimrod had arranged for someone she called a therapist to visit once a week to give him exercises to work on.

He smiled, thinking of Kira.

George smiled, thinking of strawberry juice.

And they looked out of the window together.

THE END

Look for the final part of the Princelings trilogy:

The Princelings and the Lost City

The Princelings of the East series:
     1 The Princelings of the East
     2 The Princelings and the Pirates
     3 The Princelings and the Lost City
     (these three comprise "The Trilogy", also
     available in paperback)
     4 The Traveler in Black and White
     5 The Talent Seekers
     6 Bravo Victor
     7 ....

Watch out for short stories featuring the Princelings and their friends on the Princelings website, especially around Christmas time. We may release these as an anthology, at some stage in the future.

Read more about Jemima Pett and get background to the Princelings' world on her blog jemimapett.com

Follow on Twitter @jemima_pett

The Princelings official website is at princelings.co.uk

Follow the Princelings stories on Facebook facebook.com/Princelings

Did you enjoy this book? Why not leave a review at your purchase site?

Author Jemima Pett

I've been writing stories, creating articles and event reports for newsletters and magazines ever since I was eight years, but early fiction attempts failed for want of suitable inspiration: I just couldn't find interesting characters and plot! I had a series of careers in business that kept me chained to a desk for many years. I wrote manuals, reports, science papers, blogs, journals, anything and everything that kept the words flowing. Finally, the characters jumped into my head with stories that needed to be told, and THE PRINCELINGS OF THE EAST was born.

I now live in Norfolk, England, with my six guinea pigs, successors to the originals, Fred, George, Hugo and Victor.

I am currently working on Book 7, provisionally called The Chronicles of Willoughby the Narrator.

CPSIA information can be obtained at www.ICGtesting.com
Printed in the USA
LVOW06s0132030915

452641LV00028B/617/P